AMERICAN VOICES FROM

The Time of Slavery

PRICE, BIRCH & CO
DEALERS IN SLAVES.

AMERICAN VOICES FROM

The Time of Slavery

Elizabeth Sirimarco

Marshall Cavendish Benchmark
New York

Marshall Cavendish Benchmark
99 White Plains Road
Tarrytown, New York 10591-9001
www.marshallcavendish.us

All Internet sites were available and accurate when this book was sent to press.

Library of Congress Cataloging-in-Publication Data
Sirimarco, Elizabeth, 1966–
The time of slavery / Elizabeth Sirimarco.
p. cm. — (American voices from—)
Summary: "Describes the history of slavery in the United States—from the landing of the first enslaved Africans to the close of the Civil War—through various primary source documents, such as slave narratives, advertisements, newspaper accounts, official documents and laws, plus contemporary art and photos"—Provided by publisher.
Includes bibliographical references and index.
ISBN-13: 978-0-7614-2169-6
ISBN-10: 0-7614-2169-6
1. Slavery—United States—History—Juvenile literature. 2. African Americans—History—To 1863—Juvenile literature. 3. Slavery—United States—History—Sources—Juvenile literature. 4. African Americans—History—To 1863—Sources—Juvenile literature. I. Title. II. Series.

E441.S56 2006 306.3'620973—dc22
2005025854

Printed in Malaysia
1 3 5 6 4 2

Editor: Joyce Stanton
Editorial Director: Michelle Bisson
Art Director: Anahid Hamparian
Series design and composition: Anne Scatto / PIXEL PRESS
Photo Research by Linda Sykes Picture Research, Inc., Hilton Head, S.C.

The photographs in this book are used by permission and through the courtesy of:

Los Angeles County Museum of Art: front cover; Schomburg Center for Research in Black Culture, New York Public Library: ii, 30, 33; Corbis: viii, 85; Musee des Beaux Arts, Nantes: x; National Museum of American Art/Art Resource, NY: xii; The Granger Collection, New York: xiii, xix, xx, xxii, 11, 22, 26 (both) 34, 40, 47, 51, 60, 63, 64, 66, 71, 73, 74, 77, 79 (top), 79 (bottom), 80, 83, 88, 91, 92, 95, 97 100, 108, 109; Musee de l'Homme, Paris, France/ Art Resource, NY: xiv; Karolik Collection/Museum of Fine Arts, Boston/ Bridgeman Art Library: xvii; Musee des Arts Africains et Oceaniens/Dagli Orti/The Art Archive: xxiv; Maritime Museum Kronborg Castle, Denmark/Dagli Orti/The Art Archive: 3, Royal Albert Memorial Museum, Exeter, Devon, UK/ The Bridgeman Art Library: 5; Private Collection/ ©Michael Graham-Stewart/The Bridgeman Art Library: 8; Collection of the Society of California Pioneers: 17; Chicago Historical Society: 19, 107, 108; Historical Society of Pennsylvania: 20 (both) Smithsonian American Art Museum, Washington, D. C./Art Resource, NY: 44; Carnegie Museum of Art, Pittsburgh PA: 53; Private Collection/ Art Resource, NY: 56; Abby Aldrich Rockefeller Folk Art Collection/Colonial Williamsburg: 58; Pennsylvania Academy of the Fine Arts, Philadelphia. John Lambert Fund: 87; New-York Historical Society, New York/Bridgeman Art Library: 104.

ON THE COVER: *The Cotton Pickers* by Winslow Homer, 1876

ON THE TITLE PAGE: A slave auction house in Alexandria, Virginia

TO THE SLAVES
AND THEIR DESCENDANTS,
in recognition of their lives and contributions

Contents

This 1862 photo of slaves belonging to a Confederate general is an example of a primary source that gives visual evidence of the past.

About Primary Sources

What Is a Primary Source?

In the pages that follow, you will be hearing many different "voices" from an important period in America's past. Some of the selections are long and others are short. You'll find many easy to understand at first reading, while others may require several readings. All the selections have one thing in common, however. They are primary sources. This is the name historians give to the bits and pieces of information that make up the record of human existence. Primary sources are important to us because they are the core material of all historical investigation. You might call them "history" itself.

Primary sources are evidence; they give historians the all-important clues they need to understand the past. Perhaps you have read a detective story in which a sleuth has to solve a mystery by piecing together bits of evidence he or she uncovers. The detective makes deductions, or educated guesses based on the evidence, and solves the mystery once all the deductions point in a certain direction. Historians work in much the same way. Like detectives,

This elegant painting of a French slave ship was made to commemorate a particularly successful voyage made in 1772, when only 7 of the ship's 340 captives were lost.

historians analyze the data by careful reading and rereading. After much analysis, they draw conclusions about an event, a person, or an entire era. Different historians may analyze the same evidence and come to different conclusions. That is why there is often sharp disagreement about an event.

Primary sources are also called documents. This rather dry word can be used to describe many different things: an official speech by a government leader, an old map, an act of Congress, a letter worn out from too much handling, an entry hastily scrawled in a diary, a detailed newspaper account of an event, a funny or sad song, a colorful poster, a painting, a cartoon, a faded photograph, or someone's remembrances captured on tape or film.

By examining the following documents, you the reader will be taking on the role of historian. Here is your chance to immerse yourself in a troubling era of American history: the 250 years during which slavery was part of the national landscape. You will come to know the voices of the men and women who lived through this period. You will read the words of political leaders and poets, slaves and abolitionists, rebels and writers.

The selections you will read may be difficult to understand at first. Some of the primary sources were written in a very formal style, and you may encounter challenging words and concepts. Others were written in the dialect of the slaves by people who interviewed them and hoped to capture the special ways in which they spoke. Don't let the writing put you off. Interpreting these kinds of documents is exactly the sort of work a historian does. Like a historian, when your work is done, you will have a deeper, more meaningful understanding of the past.

How to Read a Primary Source

Each document in this book deals with the history of slavery in America. Some of the documents are from government archives such as the Library of Congress. Others are from the official papers of major figures in American history, such as Frederick Douglass. Still others are taken from the narratives and autobiographies of the slaves themselves. All of the documents, major and minor, help us to understand what it was like to live during the time when slavery was legal in the United States.

As you read each document, ask yourself some basic but important questions. Who is writing or speaking? Who is that person's audience? What is he or she trying to tell that audience? Is the message clearly expressed, or is it implied, that is, stated indirectly? What words does the writer use to convey his or her message? Are the words emotional or objective in tone? If you are looking at a photograph or drawing, examine it carefully, taking in all the details. What is its content? What is its purpose? How does the photographer or artist reveal his or her feelings about the subject? These are questions that can help you think critically about a primary source.

Some tools have been included with the documents to help you in your investigations. Unusual or challenging words have been defined near the selections and in the glossary at the back of the book. Thought-provoking questions follow many of the documents. These can help focus

A photograph taken in 1850. What do you think is the relationship between the woman and child?

This 1860 engraving of slaves crowded together on the deck of the ship *Wildfire* is testimony to history. Although the slave trade had been outlawed for decades, ships like *Wildfire* continued to bring African captives to the Americas. The possible profits were worth the risk of punishment.

your reading so that you get the most out of the document. As you read the selections, you will probably come up with many questions of your own. That's great! The work of a historian always leads to many, many questions. Some can be answered, while others will require more investigation. Perhaps when you finish reading this book, your questions will lead you to further explorations about a difficult period in our history, one that some Americans would prefer to forget.

Slavery was ugly and dehumanizing, but it is a part of American history that we must face honestly.

Introduction

A NATION'S SHAME

We Americans have a lot to admire about our history. Our Founding Fathers shaped a great nation out of a noble vision—a land conceived in liberty and based upon democratic principles. Our Declaration of Independence put forth the enlightened view that all men were created equal and endowed by their Creator with "certain unalienable Rights": among these being life, liberty, and the pursuit of happiness. Ever since the Revolutionary War, American soldiers have fought for freedom, both at home and abroad. We have a lot to be proud of. But there are also aspects of our history that inspire not pride, but shame and remorse. Chief among these is slavery.

On a personal level, it isn't easy to think about difficult parts of one's past, or about embarrassing or dishonest things we may have done. In the same way, it isn't easy to think about our nation's failings. Nevertheless, it is necessary to be honest with ourselves. In considering what once went wrong, we have a better chance of doing what's right. "History is not just facts and events," says Julius Lester, author of *To Be a Slave.* "History is also a pain in the heart and we repeat history until we are able to make another's pain in the heart our own." As we study the story of slavery in America, we can think about ways to make our nation—and ourselves—stronger and more honorable. Perhaps most important, we can develop greater empathy for others, be they black or white, American or foreign.

In 1619 Dutch traders brought twenty Africans to Jamestown, Virginia, to be sold as slaves. They were the first Africans to arrive in England's American colonies for this purpose. It would be near the end of the century before Africans would become the dominant source of labor in America. At first, colonists relied more on indentured servants from England and other parts of Europe. These were people who agreed to four to seven years of servitude in exchange for passage to the New World, as well as food, shelter, and clothing during their term of service. Like slaves, indentured servants could be bought and sold; unlike slaves, they were free once they completed their contracts.

Native American slaves also supplied manpower to the colonists, but for a variety of reasons, they were never a major component of the workforce. For one, their familiarity with the land made it easier for them to escape. For another, as some historians suggest, the men viewed agriculture as "women's work" and therefore were, at best, reluctant laborers. But perhaps the most telling reason is that they simply didn't survive the European invasion. Disease, especially smallpox, ravaged the native peoples. Most scholars today agree that the number of Native Americans alive in 1619 was only 5 to 10 percent of what their population had been a century earlier. Smallpox in the seventeenth century continued to wipe out native communities throughout the colonies.

Disease not only struck down the Indians; half of the indentured servants in Maryland and Virginia lost their lives to illness within five years of their arrival. At the same time, the number of people willing to enter indentured servitude began to decrease, in part because more jobs were available in England. Such factors led to a labor crisis in the colonies—one that came at an inconvenient time. In the Southern colonies, agriculture—particularly the raising of crops such as tobacco and cotton—was beginning to make a small number of planters very wealthy. This success required significant manpower. Looking for other sources of labor, the colonists turned to

Cotton was the "king" of Southern agriculture during the 1800s. Cotton plantations like this one, painted in the 1850s by Charles Giroux, were worked entirely by slave labor.

enslaved Africans, whose farming skills made them highly prized workers. They also seemed, given the African climate, well adapted to the intense heat and humidity of the South.

Although the majority of slaves lived in the Southern colonies, slavery was not restricted to that region. In 1690, for example, one of every nine families in Boston owned a slave. The proportion was even higher in New York City; there, at around the same time, two of every five families owned a slave. What would ultimately determine the geography of slavery in America were two revolutions.

First, the Industrial Revolution brought technology that converted the North to a manufacturing economy, one that depended on machinery and the paid labor of the working class to produce goods. The region also had small, independent farms, rather than great plantations like those that dotted the South, and so did not rely as heavily on agricultural laborers.

Second, the spirit of the American Revolution inspired some citizens of the North to see slavery as inconsistent with the values of the young nation. In 1777 Vermont became the first state to abolish slavery; Pennsylvania followed three years later. Over the next twenty years all the Northern states made arrangements for the emancipation of their slaves. Abolition societies were organized throughout the region.

Hence, it was the South where slavery would leave its greatest mark and where the economy, especially after the invention of the cotton gin, would grow to depend heavily on slave labor. Invented in 1793 by Eli Whitney, the cotton gin had a tremendous impact on the production of cotton in the South—and ultimately on the practice of slavery. Cleaning the seeds from cotton by hand was a

Whitney's cotton gin made it possible to process more cotton than ever before. The gin mechanically separated cotton seeds from the valuable fibers. Without the new machine, the tightly clinging seeds would have to be picked out by hand, a wearisome, time-consuming job.

difficult and time-consuming job. Before Whitney's invention, a worker could manage to clean only about a pound of cotton a day. With the cotton gin and a few laborers, it became possible to clean fifty pounds a day; what once took a whole crew of workers a full day to accomplish could now be done in minutes. In the year of its invention, about 180,000 pounds of cotton were harvested in the United States. Two years later, that number skyrocketed to 6 million pounds. Later the gin was adapted to work with a steam engine, and by 1810 Southern farmers produced a remarkable 93 million pounds of cotton.

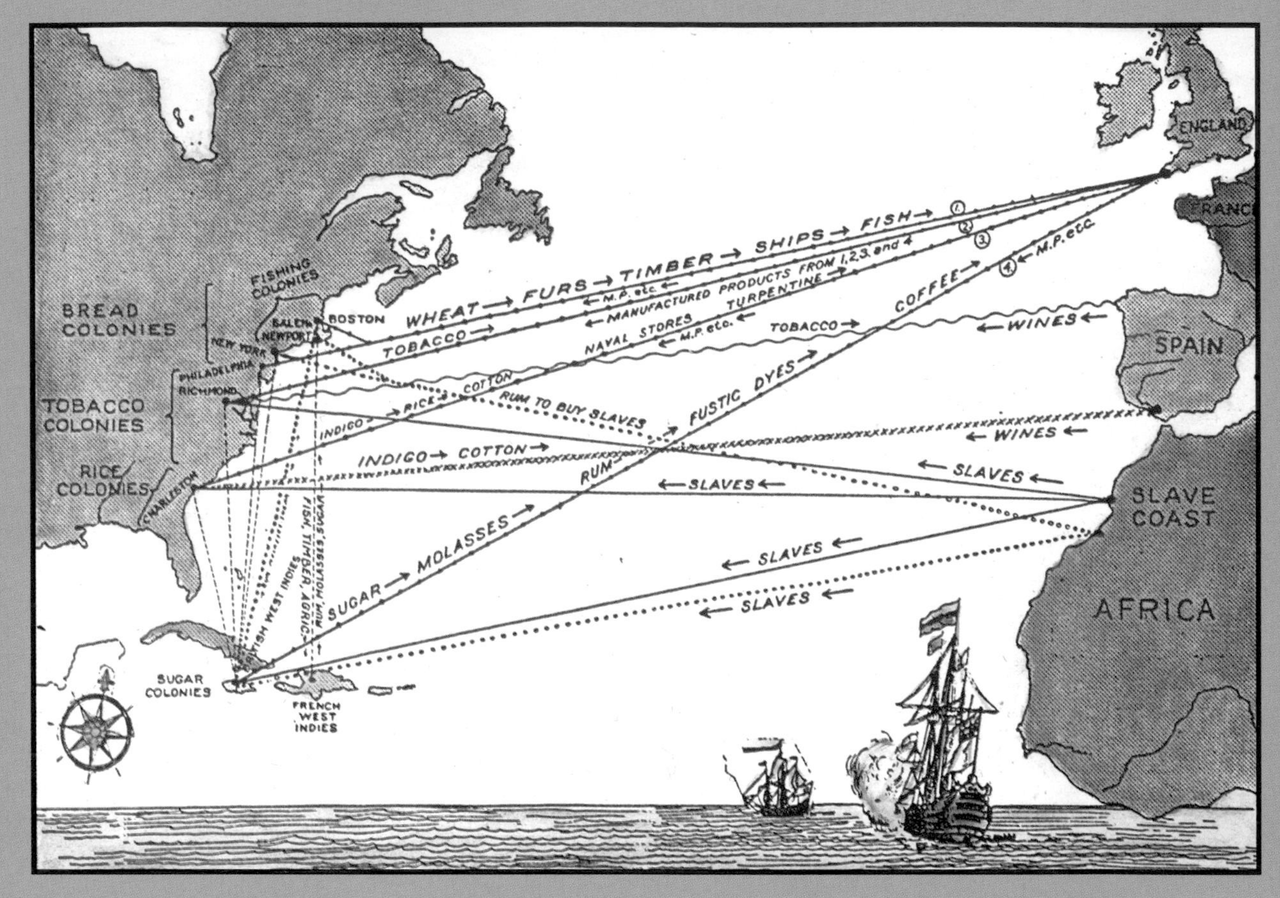

This old map shows the "trade triangle" between Africa, the Americas, and Europe in the 1600s and 1700s. As you can see, African slaves formed the basis of the whole economy.

Whitney's cotton gin single-handedly revived the sagging Southern economy. Demand for cotton increased enormously, and Southern farmers planted more and more fields of the lucrative crop. This of course required more laborers to pick and glean the cotton—work even more unpleasant than cleaning it by hand. Although the young country had seen an influx of immigrants willing to work for low wages, few were willing to take on this disagreeable job. Thus, as the rest of the nation turned away from slave labor, Southerners increasingly grew to rely on it.

Even then, however, the Northern states, and European nations as well, played significant roles in the system of slavery, providing markets where the South sold its cotton and tobacco—crops grown with the sweat and blood of slaves. Equally significant, the majority of slave traders—the merchants who transported captive Africans from their homeland to the New World—were not American, but European. And while the institution of slavery may have faded in the North, Northerners did not uniformly support emancipation or even civil rights for people of African descent. They were not immune to racism, either; while blacks in the North were free, they still did not enjoy the same rights and privileges as white citizens did.

Nevertheless, an imaginary boundary began to separate North from South, free state from slave state. Slavery began to divide the nation, literally and figuratively. By the middle of the nineteenth century, it had become an explosive political issue. The abolitionists, gaining momentum with the help of such articulate speakers as William Lloyd Garrison and Frederick Douglass, were convincing more and more people that slavery was an evil that threatened to destroy the nation. Slaveholders came up with incredible

Harriet Tubman (c. 1823–1913), one of the greatest heroes in the movement to abolish slavery

arguments to defend their position, citing the Bible or spurious science as evidence of the inferiority of African Americans. At the same time, many Northern politicians began to support "free soil"—the idea that slavery be made illegal in any new territory that opened up in the West. For their part, most Southerners believed that such a law would be unconstitutional, citing "states' rights," the idea that each individual state, rather than the federal government, had the right to make decisions about certain issues, such as slavery, that affected life within its borders.

The troubled state of the Union reached a critical point with Abraham Lincoln's election to the presidency in 1860. Lincoln was a member of the Republican Party, founded in 1854. Most early Republicans believed that the nation's interests should take precedence over those of the individual states, and many were free-soil advocates who opposed the spread of slavery. Southerners saw Lincoln's election as the beginning of the end of slavery and their world as they knew it. Determined to retain their way of life, one after another of the Southern states seceded from the Union. They formed the Confederate States of America, where slavery would remain legal until 1863, when Lincoln's Emancipation Proclamation took effect, or, in reality, until the South lost the Civil War. Then, in 1865, the United States passed the Thirteenth Amendment to the Constitution, outlawing the institution of slavery forever.

In the chapters that follow, you will read firsthand accounts of what it was like to be a slave. The slaves themselves will tell you their experiences: how they spent their days, whom they loved, what they endured, and how they risked their lives in order to reach freedom. You will read, too, selections from the laws that were enacted to protect slave owners and support the institution of slavery—laws that were also meant to instill a sense of inferiority in African Americans. You'll read shocking accounts of inhumanity. At the same time you'll experience, close up, some triumphant moments in the nation's history when "justice and freedom for all" began to include a greater proportion of the country's people.

Slaves are marched to market under the watchful eyes of their African captors.

Chapter I

From Freedom to Slavery

THERE WERE THREE LEGS on the journey into bondage for Africans destined for the New World: their capture and transport from the interior to the western coast of the African continent; their trip across the Atlantic Ocean; and their sale once they arrived in America. Although some Europeans took part in the capture and kidnapping of potential slaves, most often it was Africans who handled this step of the process. Slavery had existed in Africa long before the arrival of the Europeans, and Africans accepted the practice. It was viewed differently in Africa, however, and the treatment of slaves was generally much more humane than it would be in the Americas. As one observer noted, "They are remarkably kind to, and careful of their slaves . . . whom they treat with respect, and whom they will not suffer to be ill-used. This is a forcible lesson from the wild and savage Africans, to the more polished and enlightened Europeans who . . . treat [the slaves] as if they were a lower order of creatures, and abuse them in the most shocking manner."

The continent of Africa holds a diverse population, made up of many different peoples, and African slave traders generally did not sell people from their own tribe or homeland. Until Europeans entered the picture, the majority of the enslaved were prisoners of war or villagers captured during raids. Sometimes leaders enslaved their own subjects, usually as punishment for unpaid debts or criminal acts. Occasionally they sold their people into slavery during times of drought and famine.

Beginning in the late seventeenth century, the demand for slaves in the New World exploded, as did the money that could be made in the slave trade. This changed things dramatically for Africans on many parts of the continent. Captives could now be sent thousands of miles from their homes, not to another village within real or imagined reach of one's home and loved ones. Innocent people living in unprotected villages—young children, women, men, even the elderly—were increasingly vulnerable to unprovoked attacks and kidnappings. Spurred by greed or hoping to protect their own, rulers worked hand in hand with traders. Africans were increasingly made captive for minor debts, petty crimes, and even religious beliefs.

Once captured, the enslaved were bound together and forced to march barefoot, often for hundreds of miles, to the western coast of Africa, where European merchants, primarily from England, France, and Portugal, had set up trading posts. Many captives died on the journey to the coast. Skeletons were said to litter the roadside along the routes that the traders used. In exchange for human beings, European traders offered items such as firearms, gold, shells, alcohol, and beads.

Slaves lost not only their freedom but also their dignity and, often, their hope. On the Middle Passage, many also lost their lives owing to the cramped, unsanitary conditions in the holds of slave ships.

After purchase, the captives were prepared for the second leg of their journey. Loaded into the holds of slave ships bound for the New World, they were shackled in dark, cramped quarters without fresh air. The notorious trip across the Atlantic Ocean, known as the Middle Passage, claimed a huge number of lives. A quarter of a ship's human cargo easily might die of malnutrition and disease. Some of the captives committed suicide to escape the ships' inhumane conditions, preferring death to a life of slavery.

For those captives who made it to the New World, the final leg of the journey involved their sale. As the Africans stood in fear and confusion, New World buyers inspected them like livestock. Once purchased, most slaves were separated from any friends or family members who had made the journey with them.

From the 1520s through the 1860s, an estimated 11 to 12 million Africans were transported by force from the continent of Africa; about 600,000 of these captives ended up in the Thirteen Colonies (later the United States). Many more never made it that far. From 15 to 30 percent of captives died on the march to the coast or while waiting for weeks in the holds of European slave ships before departure on the transatlantic voyage. Some 10 to 15 percent—nearly two million more—died during the Middle Passage. The following selections offer accounts of the horrific journey from Africa to America, and from freedom to slavery.

The Interesting Narrative: Olaudah Equiano Tells of His Capture

Olaudah Equiano was among the first of many former slaves who would write about their experiences. Born in 1745 in what is now southeastern Nigeria, Equiano was the son of a chief, who himself owned slaves. Equiano was kidnapped as a young boy and lived as a slave in two African villages before European slave traders sent him to the Americas. Later sold to a merchant in the Caribbean, Equiano was given a position of responsibility that allowed him to earn a small amount of money for himself. In 1766 he was able to purchase his freedom. Equiano moved to England, where he wrote and published *The Interesting Narrative of the Life of Olaudah Equiano, or Gustavus Vassa.* (Gustavus Vassa was the name given to Equiano by one of his masters.) The book was widely read in both England and the United States. In the following passage, Equiano recalls his capture at the age of eleven.

This portrait of Olaudah Equiano was painted in England in the 1780s, about twenty years after he regained his freedom.

ONE DAY, WHEN all our people were gone out to their works as usual, and only I and my dear sister were left to mind the house, two men and a woman got over our walls, and in a moment seized us both; and, without giving us time to cry out, or make resistance, they stopped our mouths, and ran off with us into the nearest wood. Here they tied our hands, and continued to carry us as far as they could, till night came on, when we reached a small house, where the robbers halted for refreshment, and spent the night. We were then unbound; but were unable to take any food; and, being quite overpowered by fatigue and grief, our only relief was some sleep, which allayed our misfortune for a short time. The next morning we left the house and continued traveling all the day. . . . I discovered some people at a distance, on which I began to cry out for their assistance; but my cries had no other effect than to make them tie me faster, and stop my mouth, and then they put me into a large sack. They also stopped my sister's mouth, and tied her hands; and in this manner we proceeded till we were out of the sight of these people.— When we went to rest the following night they offered us some victuals [food]; but we refused them; and the only comfort we had was in being in one another's arms all that night, and bathing each other with our tears. But, alas! we were soon deprived of even the smallest comfort of weeping together. The next day proved a day of greater sorrow than I had yet experienced: for my sister and I were then separated, while we lay clasped in each other's arms. It was in vain that we besought them not to part us; she was torn from me, and immediately carried away.

". . . my cries had no other effect than to make them tie me faster."

—*From* The Interesting Narrative of the Life of Olaudah Equiano, or Gustavus Vassa, the African. Written by Himself. *Edited by Vincent Carretta. New York: Penguin Classics, 2003.*

Think about This

1. Why might the traders have chosen to kidnap children rather than adults?
2. Why do you think Equiano's family couldn't find him?

"That Horrible Place": A Captive Recollects the Middle Passage

A former slave named Mahommah G. Baquaqua was among the millions of people who experienced the indescribable misery of the Middle Passage. Baquaqua was born in the city of Zoogoo in central Africa, probably in the 1820s. Captured and sold into slavery, he was transported first to Brazil and then the United States, where he was finally able to escape from slavery. In 1854 he told his life story to Samuel Moore, who published the account. The story included a firsthand description of what it was like in the hold of a slave ship. Following is Baquaqua's recollection of the Middle Passage.

ITS HORRORS, AH! WHO CAN DESCRIBE? None can so truly depict its horrors as the poor unfortunate, miserable wretch that has been confined within its portals. . . . We were thrust into the hold of the vessel in a state of nudity, the males being crammed on one side and the females on the other; the hold was so low that we could not stand up, but were obliged to crouch upon the floor or sit down; day and night were the same to us, sleep being denied as from the confined position of our bodies, and we became desperate through suffering and fatigue.

Oh! the loathsomeness and filth of that horrible place will never be effaced from my memory; nay, as long as memory holds her seat in this distracted brain, will I remember that. My heart even at this day, sickens at the thought of it.

"Oh! the loathsomeness and filth."

Let those *humane individuals,* who are in favor of slavery, only allow themselves to take the slave's position in the noisome hold of a slave ship, just for one trip from Africa to America, and without going into the horrors of slavery further than this, if they do not come out thorough-going abolitionists, then I have no more to say in favor of abolition. . . . I imagine there can be but one place more horrible in all creation than the hold of a slave

noisome
offensive to the senses, especially the sense of smell

A slave holds up a drinking bowl to be filled from above deck as two sailors carry away a dead slave.

ship, and that place is where slaveholders . . . are the most likely to find themselves some day. . . .

The only food we had during the voyage was corn soaked and boiled. I cannot tell how long we were thus confined, but it seemed a very long while. We suffered very much for want of water, but was denied all we needed. A pint a day was all that was allowed, and no more; and a great many slaves died upon the passage. There was one poor fellow became so very desperate for want of water, that he attempted to snatch a knife from the white man who brought in the water, when he was taken up on deck and I never knew what became of him. I supposed he was thrown overboard.

refractory
disobedient

When any one of us became refractory, his flesh was cut with a knife, and pepper or vinegar was rubbed in to make him peaceable (!) I suffered, and so did the rest of us, very much from sea sickness at first, but that did not cause our brutal owners any trouble. Our sufferings were our own, we had no one to share our troubles, none to care for us, or even to speak a word of comfort to us. Some were thrown overboard before breath was out of their bodies; when it was thought any would not live, they were got rid of in that way. Only twice during the voyage were we allowed to go on deck to wash ourselves—once whilst at sea, and again just before going into port.

—From Mahommah G. Baquaqua and Samuel Moore, Biography of Mahommah G. Baquaqua, a Native of Zoogoo, in the Interior of Africa. *Detroit, MI: Geo. P. Pomeroy & Co., 1854. Available online at: http://docsouth.unc.edu/neh/baquaqua/title.html*

Think about This

Baquaqua suggests that there is only one place worse than the hold of a slave ship. Where do you think this is?

"The Sorrows of Yamba"

"The Sorrows of Yamba" tells the story of an African woman kidnapped and then sold into slavery. It is often attributed to the British poet Hannah More (1745–1833), a tireless supporter of the abolitionist movement. More was the editor of a series of inexpensive publications called the Cheap Repository Tracts, which were designed for moral and religious instruction. More may or may not have been the author of "The Sorrows of Yamba." She may have simply published the poem for another writer, perhaps even a former slave. The work first appeared in England in 1795 and was published in the United States in 1805. The following excerpt offers a poignant image of an African mother's grief.

In St. Lucie's distant Isle,
"Still with Afric's [Africa's] love I burn;
"Parted many a thousand mile,
"Never, never to return.

"Come, kind death! and give me rest,
"Yamba has no friend [but] thee;
"Thou can'st ease my throbbing breast,
"Thou can'st set the Prisoner free.

"Down my cheeks the tears are dripping,
"Broken is my heart with grief;
"Mangled my poor flesh with whipping,
"Come kind death! and bring relief.

"Come, kind death!"

"Born on Afric's Golden Coast,
"Once I was as blest as you;
"Parents tender I could boast,
"Husband dear, and children too.

"Whity Man he came from far,
"Sailing o'er the briny flood,
"Who, with help of British Tar,
"Buys up human flesh and blood.

tar
sailor

"With the Baby at my breast;
"(Other two were sleeping by)
"In my Hut I sat at rest
"With no thought of danger nigh.

This 1832 illustration comments on the fact that many nineteenth-century Americans idealized white women while treating black women as property.

"From the bush at even tide
    "Rush'd the fierce man-stealing Crew;
"Seiz'd the Children by my side,
    "Seiz'd the wretched Yamba too.

"Then for love of filthy Gold,
    "Strait they bore me to the sea;
"Cramm'd me down a Slave-ship's hold,
    "Where were Hundreds stow'd like me.

"Naked on the platform lying,
    "Now we cross the tumbling wave;
"Shrieking, sickening, fainting, dying,
    "Deed of shame for Britons brave.

. . .

"I in groaning pass'd the night,
    "And did roll my aching head;
"At the break of morning light,
    "My poor Child was cold and dead.

"Happy, happy there she lies!
    "Thou shalt feel the lash no more.
"Thus full many a Negro dies,
    "Ere we reach the destin'd shore.

"Driven like Cattle to a fair,
    "See they sell us young and old;
"Child from Mother too they tear,
    "All for love of filthy Gold.

"I was sold to Massa [master] hard,
    "Some have Massas kind and good;
"And again my back was scarr'd
    "Bad and stinted was my food.

"Poor and wounded, faint and sick,
    "All exposs'd to burning sky,
"Massa bids me grass to pick,
    "And now I am near to die. . . ."

—From Hannah More (attributed), "The Sorrows of Yamba or The Negro Woman's Lamentation," in The Longman Anthology of British Literature. *Vol. 2A,* The Romantics and Their Contemporaries. *Upper Saddle River, NJ: Addison Wesley Longman. Original work published in the Cheap Repository Tracts, 1795.*

Think about This

1. How does Yamba feel about death? How would she have compared it to slavery?
2. Yamba's children were also kidnapped. What happened to them?

A Broadside Announces New Arrivals

The atrocious conditions under which the African captives were transported helped make health concerns important to traders and slave owners alike. One infected individual could cause an epidemic with serious consequences to plantation life, not to mention the damage to profits. To lessen the risks, new arrivals from Africa were often quarantined for a period of time before being put up for auction. Other measures, such as cleaning or fumigating the ships, might also be taken. In the following broadside, or large printed advertisement, merchants reassure potential buyers at an upcoming auction that their "cargo" is free from smallpox.

CHARLESTOWN, April 27, 1769

TO BE SOLD,

On Wednesday the Tenth Day of
May next,

A CHOICE CARGO OF
Two Hundred & Fifty
NEGROES:

ARRIVED in the Ship
Countess of Sussex, Thomas Davies,
Master, directly from Gambia, by
JOHN CHAPMAN, & Co.

THIS is the Vessel that had the Small-Pox on Board at the Time of her Arrival the 31st of March last: Every necessary Precaution hath since been taken to cleanse both Ship and Cargo thoroughly, so that those who may be inclined to purchase need not be under the least Apprehension of Danger from Infliction.

The NEGROES are allowed to be the likeliest Parcel that have been imported this Season.

allowed *thought*

likeliest *most promising*

—From broadside of April 27, 1769, Charleston, South Carolina. Worchester, MA: American Antiquarian Society.

Think about This

1. What emotions does this broadside stir in you? What thoughts does it evoke?
2. Can you put yourself in the mind-set of the eighteenth-century slaveholder?

Chapter 2

Slavery: A Legal Right

AT FIRST THE COLONIES HAD no strict laws governing the rights of slaves and their owners. It was unclear, for example, whether a slave could ever become free, or whether his or her child was a slave from birth. But as the practice of slavery spread, the colonists began to enact legislation to protect their investments. Chief among these were laws stating that, unlike indentured servants, slaves served for life, with little or no chance to attain freedom.

As slavery spread, so, too, did the variety of laws that controlled the slaves and protected the slaveholders. These laws touched on every aspect of slaves' lives, often barring them from marrying, practicing religion, or learning to read and write. Laws also governed the severity of punishment that slaves could face, for everything from minor infractions such as disobedience to the larger crime of trying to escape. In this chapter, you will explore some of the slave laws that governed first the colonies and then the United States.

From almost the beginning of slavery in America, relationships between slaves and slaveholders could be complex and close. This nineteenth-century photograph is testimony to the generations of white children who were raised by African-American nannies and governesses.

A Virginia Law Defines Slaves' Status

In 1705 the Virginia general assembly enacted a law that confirmed a slave's status as property. Soon similar legislation would be enacted in other colonies as well. Following is a portion of the law.

Sale of Slaves and Stock.

The Negroes and Stock listed below, are a Prime Lot, and belong to the ESTATE OF THE LATE LUTHER McGOWAN, and will be sold on Monday, Sept. 22nd, 1852, at the Fair Grounds, in Savannah, Georgia, at 1:00 P. M. The Negroes will be taken to the grounds two days previous to the Sale, so that they may be inspected by prospective buyers.

On account of the low prices listed below, they will be sold for cash only, and must be taken into custody within two hours after sale.

No.	Name.	Age.	Remarks.	Price.
1	Lunesta	27	Prime Rice Planter,	$1,275.00
2	Violet	16	Housework and Nursemaid,	900.00
3	Lizzie	30	Rice, Unsound,	300.00
4	Minda	27	Cotton, Prime Woman,	1,200.00
5	Adam	28	Cotton, Prime Young Man,	1,100.00
6	Abel	41	Rice Hand, Eyesight Poor,	675.00
7	Tanney	22	Prime Cotton Hand,	950.00
8	Flementina	39	Good Cook, Stiff Knee,	400.00
9	Lanney	34	Prime Cottom Man,	1,000.00
10	Sally	10	Handy in Kitchen,	675.00
11	Maccabey	35	Prime Man, Fair Carpenter,	980.00
12	Dorcas Judy	25	Seamstress, Handy in House,	800.00
13	Happy	60	Blacksmith,	575.00
14	Mowden	15	Prime Cotton Boy,	700.00
15	Bills	21	Handy with Mules,	900.00
16	Theopolis	39	Rice Hand, Gets Fits,	575.00
17	Coolidge	29	Rice Hand and Blacksmith,	1,275.00
18	Bessie	69	Infirm, Sews,	250.00
19	Infant	1	Strong Likely Boy	400.00
20	Samson	41	Prime Man, Good with Stock,	975.00
21	Callie May	27	Prime Woman, Rice,	1,000.00
22	Honey	14	Prime Girl, Hearing Poor,	850.00
23	Angelina	16	Prime Girl, House or Field,	1,000.00
24	Virgil	21	Prime Field Hand,	1,100.00
25	Tom	40	Rice Hand, Lame Leg,	750.00
26	Noble	11	Handy Boy,	900.00
27	Judge Lesh	55	Prime Blacksmith,	800.00
28	Booster	43	Fair Mason, Unsound,	600.00
29	Big Kate	37	Housekeeper and Nurse,	950.00
30	Melie Ann	19	Housework, Smart Yellow Girl,	1,250.00
31	Deacon	26	Prime Rice Hand,	1,000.00
32	Coming	19	Prime Cotton Hand,	1,000.00
33	Mabel	47	Prime Cotton Hand,	800.00
34	Uncle Tim	60	Fair Hand with Mules,	600.00
35	Abe	27	Prime Cotton Hand,	1,000.00
36	Tennes	29	Prime Rice Hand and Cocahman,	1,250.00

There will also be offered at this sale, twenty head of Horses and Mules with harness, along with thirty head of Prime Cattle. Slaves will be sold separate, or in lots, as best suits the purchaser. Sale will be held rain or shine.

An advertisement announcing the sale of "a Prime Lot" of slaves, who are up for auction as a result of the death of their owner. As his "real estate," they're simply part of the property he left behind.

An act declaring the Negro, Mulatto [mixed race], and Indian slaves within this dominion, to be real estate.

. . . Be it enacted, by the governor, council and burgesses of this present general assembly, and it is hereby enacted by the authority of the same; That from and after the passing of this act, all negro, mulatto, and Indian slaves . . . shall be held, taken, and adjudged, to be real estate . . . and shall descend unto the heirs and widows of persons departing this life, according to the manner and custom of land of inheritance.

—From William Waller Hening, October 1705 —4th Anne, Chap XXIII, 3.333, in The Statutes at Large; Being a Collection of all the Laws of Virginia, from the First Session of the Legislature in the Year 1619. *Vol. 1. New York: R & W & G. Bartow, 1823. Available online at: http://www.law.du.edu/russell/lh/alh/docs/virginiaslaverystatutes.html*

Think about This

1. Consider what the term *real estate* usually means. What is the significance of calling a human being "real estate"?
2. According to this law, what happens to a slave upon the death of his or her owner?

"Every Such Slave Shall Suffer Death": The South Carolina Slave Code

The Negro Law of 1740, also known as the South Carolina Slave Code, was enacted in the colony of South Carolina following a series of slave revolts in the 1730s. The law applied to all "people of color" who were slaves, including Native Americans and those of mixed race. In addition to declaring that all slaves in the colony were "forever and hereafter slaves," the South Carolina code prohibited slaves from being taught how to read and write and how to raise livestock. While setting down rules about how slaves could be punished, it also addressed how whites would be disciplined for abusing their property. Following are portions of the law.

IF ANY SLAVE IN THIS PROVINCE SHALL commit any crime or offence whatsoever, which by the laws of England, or of this Province, now in force, is or has been made felony . . . every such slave, being duly convicted according to the directions of this act, shall suffer death. . . .

Any slave who shall be guilty of homicide of any sort upon

EDUCATIONAL LAWS OF VIRGINIA.

THE
PERSONAL NARRATIVE
OF
Mrs. Margaret Douglass,
A SOUTHERN WOMAN,
WHO WAS IMPRISONED FOR ONE MONTH
IN THE
COMMON JAIL OF NORFOLK,
UNDER THE LAWS OF VIRGINIA,
FOR THE CRIME OF
TEACHING FREE COLORED CHILDREN TO READ.

"Search the Scriptures!"
"How can one read unless he be taught?"
HOLY BIBLE.

BOSTON:
PUBLISHED BY JOHN P. JEWETT & CO.
CLEVELAND, OHIO:
JEWETT, PROCTOR & WORTHINGTON.
1854.

In many states it was a crime not only to teach slaves to read and write, but to educate free blacks as well. Margaret Douglass was one of many people who risked imprisonment to help African-American children learn to read.

any white person, except by misadventure, or in defence of his master . . . shall upon conviction thereof as aforesaid, suffer death. And every slave who shall raise or attempt to raise an insurrection in this Province . . . shall upon conviction as aforesaid, suffer death. . . .

. . .

BE IT ENACTED, that if any person shall wilfully murder his own slave, or the slaves of any other person, every such person shall, upon conviction thereof, forfeit and pay the sum of seven hundred pounds. . . .

If any person shall, on a sudden heat or passion, or by undue correction, kill his own slave, or the slave of any other person, he shall forfeit the sum of three hundred and fifty pounds. . . .

In case any person shall wilfully cut out the tongue, put out the eye, castrate, or cruelly scald, burn, or deprive any slave of any limb or member, or shall inflict any other cruel punishment, other than by whipping, or beating with a horsewhip, cowskin, switch, or small stick, or by putting irons on, or confining or imprisoning such slave, every such person shall, for every such offense, forfeit the sum of one hundred pounds, current money.

—*Cited by William Goodell,* The American Slave Code in Theory and Practice: Its Distinctive Features Shown by Its Statutes, Judicial Decisions, and Illustrative Facts. *New York: American and Foreign Anti-Slavery Society, 1853. Available online at: http://www.dinsdoc.com/goodell-1-0a.htm*

Think about This

1. The law describes two penalties for murdering a slave. What is the difference between them?
2. Consider the punishment a slave would receive for murdering a white person versus that which a slave owner would receive for murdering his slave or someone else's. Why do you think the penalties were so different? Do you think that the penalties for the slave owners were strong enough to protect the slaves?
3. Is there any case in which a slave would not be put to death for killing a white person?

The Constitution: Silent Approval

The existence of slavery in a young nation founded on democratic principles seems like a contradiction to us today. When the Founding Fathers drew up the Constitution in 1787, did they have anything to say about slavery? Although the words *slave* and *slavery* are never mentioned in the document, the institution is acknowledged. Consider the following passages from the Constitution and how they relate to slavery.

In 1940, when Howard Chandler Christy painted this scene of the signing of the Constitution, slavery had been abolished for seventy-five years, but most African Americans still did not enjoy full civil rights.

ARTICLE I, SECTION 2

Clause 3: Representatives and direct Taxes shall be apportioned among the several States . . . according to their respective Numbers [according to a state's population], which shall be determined by adding to the whole Number of free Persons, including those bound to Service for a Term of Years, and excluding Indians not taxed, three fifths of all other Persons.

ARTICLE I, SECTION 9

Clause 1: The Migration or Importation of such Persons as any of the States now existing shall think proper to admit, shall not be prohibited by the Congress prior to the Year one thousand eight hundred and eight, but a Tax or duty may be imposed on such Importation, not exceeding ten dollars for each Person.

ARTICLE IV, SECTION 9
Clause 3: No Person held to Service or Labour in one State, under the Laws thereof, escaping into another, shall, in Consequence of any Law or Regulation therein, be discharged from such Service or Labour, but shall be delivered up on Claim of the Party to whom such Service or Labour may be due.

—From the Constitution of the United States, adopted by a convention of the States on September 17, 1787. Full text available online at: http://memory.loc.gov/const/const.html

Think about This

1. The first passage says that the states will be taxed according to how many people reside within them. Does a slave count as a person in the population of a state?
2. Why might the Founding Fathers have put a time limit (1808) on the importation of slaves?
3. According to the last passage, if a slave escaped to a state where slavery was illegal, would he or she be free?
4. Do you think the writers of the Constitution had qualms about the institution of slavery?

In Perpetuity: Generations of Slavery

Many slave owners argued that because slavery was legal, they did nothing wrong in holding slaves or in perpetuating the institution. In 1853 a New York minister and abolitionist named William

Goodell wrote *The American Slave Code in Theory and Practice* to refute this belief. Goodell argued that the laws protecting slavery should not be respected because slavery was essentially immoral—an act against God. In the following passage, Goodell describes a feature common to all the slave codes, one that ensured the continuation of slavery with each generation.

SLAVES BEING HELD AS PROPERTY, like other domestic animals, their Offspring are held as Property, in perpetuity, in the same manner.

THE law of South Carolina says of slaves, "All their issue and their offspring, born or to be born, shall be, and are hereby declared to be, and remain FOR EVER HEREAFTER, absolute slaves, and shall follow the condition of the mother." . . .

"... FOR EVER HEREAFTER, absolute slaves."

In Maryland, "All negroes and other slaves, already imported or hereafter to be imported into this province, and all children, now born or hereafter to be born of such negroes and slaves, shall be slaves during their natural lives." . . .

Similar in Georgia. . . . And in Mississippi. . . . And in Virginia. . . . And in Kentucky. . . . And in Louisiana. . . . In all these laws it is laid down that the child follows the condition of the mother, whoever the father may be! The same usage, whether with or without written law, prevails in all our slave States; and under its sanction, the slave "owner" very frequently holds and sells his own children as "property," though sometimes as white as himself.

"That is property which the law declares TO BE property. Two hundred years of legislation have sanctified and sanctioned negro slaves as property." (HENRY CLAY; Speech, U.S. Senate, 1839.)

So also Mr. Gholson, in the Legislature of Virginia: "The owner of land has a reasonable right to its annual produce, the owner of brood mares to their products, and the owner of female slaves to their increase [offspring]."

Thus the perpetuity of slavery grows out of its hereditary transmission. . . . The duty of a future liberation would imply the unlawfulness of present possession. Intelligent slaveholders, perceiving this, are careful to fortify their present claims upon human chattels, by enactments seeking the perpetuity of the system.

—From William Goodell, "The Relation Hereditary and Perpetual." Chap. 21 in The American Slave Code in Theory and Practice: Its Distinctive Features Shown by Its Statutes, Judicial Decisions, and Illustrative Facts. *New York: American and Foreign Anti-Slavery Society, 1853. Available online at: http://www.dinsdoc.com/goodell-1-1-21.htm*

Think about This

1. Why do these laws apply to children born to slave women but say nothing about the fathers of the children?
2. To what does the Virginia legislator Mr. Gholson compare the children of slaves?
3. Carefully consider the following sentence: "The duty of a future liberation would imply the unlawfulness of present possession." What does Goodell mean by this?

Thomas Jefferson: Abolitionist and Slave Owner

Several of the Founding Fathers held slaves, and of these men none presents such a paradox as Thomas Jefferson. Recognizing that

Thomas Jefferson lavished years of care on building and improving Monticello, his Virginia estate—which was worked by slaves, in spite of Jefferson's commitment to the ideals of liberty.

slavery was a grave problem in the new nation, one that would only grow more dangerous as years passed, Jefferson himself never freed his slaves. He also believed that, should the slaves ever be emancipated, whites and blacks could never live together peacefully. "Deep rooted prejudices entertained by the whites," Jefferson noted, "ten thousand recollections, by the blacks, of the injuries they have sustained . . . and many other circumstances will divide us into parties, and produce convulsions which will probably never end but in the extermination of one or the other race." Still, Jefferson tried several times to enact laws that would emancipate the slaves, both before and after the Revolution, in Virginia and in the nation as a whole. When writing the Declaration of Independence, Jefferson had included a section condemning King George III of England for his support of slavery through the slave trade. Congress decided to eliminate the section when Georgia and South Carolina protested. Following is the portion that was eliminated from Jefferson's "original Rough draught."

"He has waged cruel war against human nature itself."

HE [KING GEORGE] HAS WAGED cruel war against human nature itself, violating it's [*sic*] most sacred rights of life & liberty in the persons of a distant people who never offended him, captivating & carrying them into slavery in another hemisphere, or to incur miserable death in their transportation thither. this piratical warfare, the opprobrium of infidel powers, is the warfare of the CHRISTIAN king of Great Britain. determined to keep open a market where MEN should be bought & sold, he has . . . [suppressed] every legislative attempt to prohibit or to restrain this execrable commerce: and . . . he is now exciting those very people to rise in arms among us, and to purchase that liberty of which he has deprived them, & murdering the people upon whom he also obtruded them; thus paying off former

opprobrium *something that brings disgrace*

execrable *detestable*

obtruded *forced*

crimes committed against the liberties of one people, with crimes which he urges them to commit against the lives of another.

—From Jefferson's "original Rough draught" of the Declaration of Independence. The Papers of Thomas Jefferson. *Vol. 1, 1760–1776. Ed. Julian P. Boyd. Princeton: Princeton University Press, 1950. The entire document is available on the Library of Congress Web site: http://www.loc.gov/exhibits/declara/ruffdrft.html*

Think about This

1. Why did Jefferson believe that the king was responsible for slavery?
2. According to Jefferson, what was the king encouraging the slaves to do? Why?
3. Does Jefferson hold the colonists to account in any way?

An End to the Slave Trade

In 1808, as the U.S. Constitution had stipulated, importation of slaves from Africa became illegal. Following is the legislation enacted by Congress.

BE IT ENACTED BY THE SENATE AND HOUSE of Representatives of the United States of America in Congress assembled, That from and after the first day of January, one thousand eight hundred and eight, it shall not be lawful to import or bring into the United States or the territories thereof from any foreign kingdom, place, or country, any negro, mulatto, or person of colour, with intent to hold, sell, or dispose of such negro, mulatto, or person of colour, as a slave, or to be held to service or labour.

—An Act to Prohibit the Importation of Slaves, approved March 7, 1807. Available online at: http://teachingamericanhistory.org/library/index.asp?document=179

Think about This

1. The slave trade was very profitable. Why do you think Americans decided to outlaw it?
2. What impact do you think this law had on the slaves in America? Do you think it had any negative effects? Positive effects?

Thousands of freed slaves wrote of their experiences or told their stories to journalists and other writers, thus leaving us a valuable record of life under slavery.

Chapter 3

Slave Narratives: Men Tell Their Stories

WHAT WAS IT LIKE TO BE A SLAVE? There is a rich collection of writings from and interviews with the slaves that can answer this question. Olaudah Equiano, whose work you read in chapter 1, is said to have written the first slave autobiography. With it, he began an important African-American literary tradition: the slave narrative.

Historians believe that some six thousand published narratives exist today. Some of these, like that of Equiano as well as the famous works of Frederick Douglass (*Narrative of the Life of Frederick Douglass*) and Harriet Jacobs (*Incidents in the Life of a Slave Girl*) are book-length autobiographies. These works became powerful tools in the abolitionists' war on slavery, for how better to describe the horrors of the institution than in the words of the slaves themselves?

Other narratives are transcribed from interviews with slaves or are brief accounts of slave life told to reporters, who then published them in abolitionist newspapers. These often tell the stories of former slaves who, never having learned to read or write, could not author their own works. Both touching and appalling, they describe the day-to-day experience of people who lived in bondage. Many of these were recorded long after the slaves were free, even into the first decades of the twentieth century.

There are a few things to consider when examining the slave narratives. Sometimes they include words that we consider offensive today, such as *nigger.* Keep in mind that the slaves used words that were common in their day. The narratives offer an example of how language, as well as our thinking, has changed since that time. Also, some of the stories may be difficult to read at first, since the interviewers tried to capture the speakers' dialects—the special ways that they used language. One historian, Bruce Fort of the University of Virginia, suggests the following: "Try to imagine what the language might have sounded like, perhaps by reading the narratives out loud."

However you read the narratives, they will leave you with a lasting impression of what it was like to live as a slave. You'll see that along with the hardships they endured, many African Americans were able to discover a sense of humanity and joy. They were human beings like any other—they fell in love and married, told jokes and argued, had children and grew old.

In the two chapters that follow, listen closely as the people tell their stories. Their narratives offer reliable, firsthand portraits. With such powerful resources as testament, the history of slavery in the United States will never be overlooked or oversimplified.

Solomon Northrup: "No Such Thing as Rest"

Born a free man in New York, Solomon Northrup was kidnapped and sold into slavery at age thirty-three, leaving behind a wife and three children. An accomplished violinist, Northrup had been lured to Washington, DC, on the promise of finding work as a professional musician there. Upon his arrival, he was beaten, drugged, and sent to Louisiana—and into slavery. It would be twelve years before he regained his freedom. Here Northrup describes a typical day on a plantation where he worked.

EIGHTH THOUSAND.

TWELVE YEARS A SLAVE.

NARRATIVE

OF

SOLOMON NORTHUP,

A CITIZEN OF NEW-YORK,

KIDNAPPED IN WASHINGTON CITY IN 1841,

AND

RESCUED IN 1853,

FROM A COTTON PLANTATION NEAR THE RED RIVER, IN LOUISIANA.

AUBURN:
DERBY AND MILLER.
BUFFALO:
DERBY, ORTON AND MULLIGAN.
LONDON:
SAMPSON LOW, SON & COMPANY, 47 LUDGATE HILL.
1853.

The title page of Solomon Northrup's narrative misspells his name but nevertheless outlines the trials undergone by this freeborn African American.

THE HANDS ARE REQUIRED to be in the cotton field as soon as it is light in the morning, and, with the exception of ten or fifteen minutes, which is given them at noon to swallow their allowance of cold bacon, they are not permitted to be a moment idle until it is too dark to see, and when the moon is full, they often times labor till the middle of the night. They do not dare to stop even at dinner time, nor return to the quarters, however late it be, until the order to halt is given by the driver.

The day's work over in the field, the baskets are . . . carried to the gin-house, where the cotton is weighed. . . . a slave never approaches the gin-house with his basket of cotton but with fear. If it falls short in weight—if he has not

gin
cotton gin

Two women slaves hoe a newly cleared field under the watchful gaze of an overseer.

performed the full task appointed him, he knows that he must suffer. And if he has exceeded it by ten or twenty pounds, in all probability his master will measure the next day's task accordingly. So, whether he has two little or too much, his approach to the gin-house is always with fear and trembling. . . . After weighing, follow the whippings; and then the baskets are carried to the cotton house. . . .

This done, the labor of the day is not yet ended, by any means. Each one must then attend to his respective chores. One feeds the mules, another the swine—another cuts the wood, and so forth. . . . Finally, at a late hour, they reach the quarters, sleepy and overcome with the long day's toil. Then a fire must be kindled in the cabin, the corn ground in the small hand-mill, and supper, and dinner for the next day in the field, prepared. . . .

". . . the fears and labors of another day begin."

An hour before day light the horn is blown. . . . It is an offense invariably followed by a flogging, to be found at the quarters after daybreak. Then the fears and labors of another day begin; and until its close there is no such thing as rest.

—From Solomon Northrup, Twelve Years a Slave: Narrative of Solomon Northrup. *Auburn, NY: Derby and Miller, 1853.*

Think about This

Why did a slave have to be careful not to pick too much cotton?

Francis Henderson: "A Matter of Necessity"

Slaves were afforded the bare minimum in terms of life's necessities. Although expected to withstand backbreaking labor from dawn until well after dusk, many owners scarcely gave their field slaves enough food to sustain them. Quarters for the enslaved were often cold and drafty, with leaky roofs; the dirt floors turned to mud in times of rain. Some slaves weren't given shoes, and most had no more than a few items of clothing to protect them from icy winters or the blazing sun of a Southern summer. In the following passage, Francis Henderson describes what life was like on the plantation where he lived, outside Washington, DC.

OUR HOUSES WERE BUT LOG HUTS—the tops partly open—rain would come through. . . . everything would be dirty and muddy. . . . My bed and bedstead consisted of a board wide enough to sleep on—one end on a stool, the other placed near the fire. My pillow consisted of my jacket—my covering was whatever I could get. My bedtick [mattress] was the board itself. . . . I only remember having but one blanket from my owners up to the age of nineteen, when I ran away.

peck *a unit of dry measure equal to eight quarts*

Our allowance was given weekly—a peck of sifted corn meal, a dozen and a half herrings, two and a half pounds of pork. Some of the boys would eat this up in three days—then they had to steal, or they could not perform their daily tasks. . . . I do not remember one slave but who stole some things—they were driven to it as a matter of necessity. I myself did this—many a time have I, with others, run among the stumps in chase of a sheep, that we might have something to eat. . . . In regard to cooking, sometimes many have to cook at one fire, and before all could get to the fire to bake hoe cakes, the overseer's horn would sound: then they must go at any rate. Many a time I have gone along eating a piece of bread and meat, or herring broiled on the coals—I never sat down at a table to eat except at harvest time.

". . . they had to steal, or they could not perform their daily tasks."

. . . In harvest time, the cooking is done at the great house, as the hands they have are wanted in the field. This was more like people, and we liked it, for we sat down then at meals.

—*From* African American Voices: The Life Cycle of Slavery, *2d ed., edited by Steve Mintz. Naugatuck, CT: Brandywine Press, 1999.*

Richard Toler: "No Good Times till Ah Was Free"

The following is one of the interviews conducted by the Federal Writers' Project during the Great Depression. Between 1936 and 1938 writers, funded by the government, interviewed more than 2,300 former slaves in seventeen states. These interviews offered the ex-slaves an opportunity to tell their stories—an opportunity they might not otherwise have had. Following is the narrative of Richard Toler, who had been a slave in Virginia during the Civil War.

AH NEVER HAD NO GOOD TIMES TILL AH WAS FREE. . . . Ah was bo'n on Mastah Tolah's [Master Toler's] plantation down in ole V'ginia. . . . we lived in a cabin way back of the big house, me and mah pappy and mammy and two brothahs.

Ah never went to school. Learned to read and write my name after ah was free in night school, but they [the masters] nevah allowed us to have a book in ouah [our] hand, and we couldn't have no money neither. If we had money we had to tu'n it ovah to ouah ownah. Chu'ch was not allowed. . . .

We was nevah allowed no pa'ties, and when they had goin' ons at the big house, we had to clear out. Ah had to wo'k hard all the time every day in the week. Had to min' the cows and calves, and when ah got older ah had to hoe in the field. . . . Ah've done about evahthing in mah life, blacksmith and stone mason, ca'penter, evahthing but brick-layin'. . . .

Befo' the wah we never had no good times. They took good care of us, though. As pa'taculah [particular] with slave as with the stock. . . . And if we claimed bein' sick, they'd give us a dose of castah oil and tu'pentine [castor oil and turpentine]. That was the principal medicine cullud [colored] folks had to take, and sometimes salts. . . . And if we was real sick, they had the Doctah fo' us.

We had very bad eatin'. Bread, meat, water. And they fed it to us in a trough, jes' like the hogs. And ah went in [my] shirt till I was 16, nevah had no clothes. And the flo' in ouah cabin was dirt, and at night we'd jes' take a blanket and lay down on the flo'. The dog was supe'ior to us; they would take him in the house.

I sho' is glad I ain't no slave no moah.

—From interview with Mr. Richard Toler, ex-slave of the Civil War period. Interviewed by Ruth Thompson, no date. WPA Slave Narrative Project, Ohio Narratives. *Vol. 12. Available online at: http://memory.loc.gov/ammem/snhtml/snhome.html*

Frederick Douglass and Moses Roper: The Marks Still Remain

The hardships of slavery were many. The psychological wear and tear of being treated as less than human, of having no control over one's life, the unending labor, the restrictive rules and regulations, the fear of losing one's family—all these factors merged to make a slave's life one of great difficulty. Added to that was the brutal physical punishment many slaves received. Following are two accounts of the inhumane treatment to which some slaves were subjected. In the first, abolitionist and escaped slave Frederick Douglass details the myriad reasons why a slave might be punished. The second is an excerpt from the autobiography of Moses Roper, who describes what happened to him when he tried to escape.

A MERE LOOK, WORD, OR MOTION,—a mistake, accident, or want of power,—are all matters for which a slave may be whipped at any time. Does a slave look dissatisfied? It is said, he has the devil in him, and it must be whipped out. Does he speak loudly when spoken to by his master? Then he is getting high-minded, and should be taken down a button-hole lower. Does he forget to pull off his hat at the approach of a white person? Then he is wanting in reverence, and should be whipped for it. Does he ever venture to vindicate his conduct, when censured for it? Then he is guilty of impudence,—one of the greatest crimes of which a slave can be guilty. Does he ever venture to suggest a different mode of doing things from that pointed out by his master? He is indeed presumptuous, and getting above himself.

". . . he has the devil in him, and it must be whipped out."

—From Frederick Douglass, Narrative of the Life of Frederick Douglass, An American Slave. *In* The Classic Slave Narratives, *edited by Henry Louis Gates, Jr. New York: Signet Classic, 2002. Original work first published in 1845.*

MY MASTER GAVE ME A HEARTY DINNER, the best he ever did give me; but it was to keep me from dying before he had given me all the flogging he intended. After dinner he took me up to the log-house, stripped me

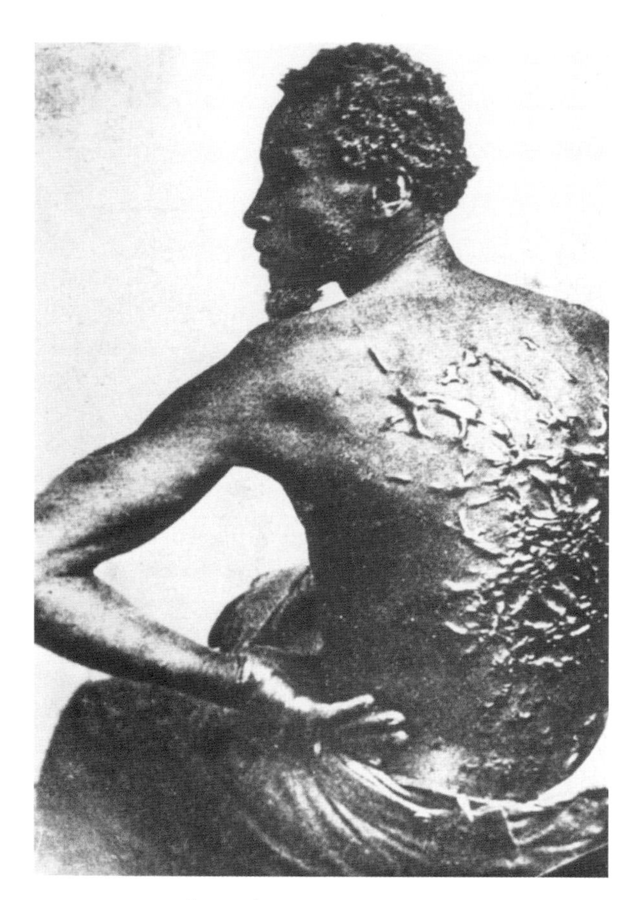

A man named Gordon, photographed not long after emancipation, shows the scars from the many whippings he endured as a slave.

quite naked, fasted a rail up very high, tied my hands to the rail, fastened my feet together, put a rail between my feet, and stood on the end of it to hold me down; the two sons then gave me fifty lashes each, the son-in-law another fifty, and Mr. Gooch himself fifty more.

. . . After this, they took me to the blacksmith's shop, got two large bars of iron, which they bent around my feet, each bar weighing twenty pounds, and put a heavy log-chain on my neck. . . .

. . . After this . . . I stayed with him several months, and did my work very well. It was about the beginning of 1832, when he took off my irons, and being in dread of him, he having threatened me with more punishment, I attempted again to escape from him. At this time I got into North Carolina: but a reward having been offered for me, a Mr. Robinson caught me, and chained me to a chair, upon which he sat up with me all night, and next day proceeded home with me. This was Saturday. Mr. Gooch had gone to church, several miles from his house. When he came back,the first thing he did was to pour some tar upon my head, then rubbed it all over my face, took a torch with pitch on, and set it on fire; he put it out before it did me very great injury, but the pain which I endured was the most excruciating, nearly all my hair having been burnt off. On Monday, he puts irons on me again, weighing nearly fifty pounds. He threatened me again on the Sunday with another flogging; and on the Monday morning, before daybreak, I got away again, with my irons on, and was about three hours going a distance of two miles. I had gone a good distance, when I met with a coloured man, who got some wedges, and took my irons off. However, I was caught again, and put into prison in Charlotte, where Mr. Gooch came, and took me back to Chester. He asked me how I got my irons off. They having been got off by a slave, I would not answer his question, for fear of getting the man punished. Upon this he put the fingers of my hands into a vice, and squeezed all the nails off. He then had my feet put on an anvil, and ordered a man to beat my toes, till he smashed some of my nails off. The marks of this treatment still remain upon me, some of my nails never having grown perfect since.

". . . he put the fingers of my hands into a vice, and squeezed all the nails off."

—*From Moses Roper,* Narrative of the Adventures and Escape of Moses Roper. *Berwick-upon-Tweed: published for the author, and printed at the Warder Office, 1848. Available online at: http://docsouth.unc.edu/neh/roper/menu.html.*

Think about This

Place yourself in Moses Roper's situation. Knowing what might happen if you were caught, would you have tried to escape?

Moses Grandy: "I Loved Her as I Loved My Life"

Most slaves lived in nuclear families—a mother, a father, and children—but these families faced a constant threat of separation. No state laws recognized marriage between slaves, and owners, not parents, held legal authority over slave children. Among the numerous difficulties that slaves endured, perhaps none was so painful as the forced separation of family members—husband from wife, mother from child. A husband could be sold from his plantation to another hundreds of miles away, a mother put up for auction at the whim of the slave owner. Perhaps he needed money or sought to punish a slave; whatever the reason, once separated, family members were unlikely to see each other again. In the following account, Moses Grandy describes the day his wife was sold. Grandy, born in North Carolina around 1786, escaped from slavery in 1833. With the help of the American Anti-Slavery Society, he published his autobiography in 1843.

I MARRIED A SLAVE BELONGING TO ENOCH SAWYER. . . . I left her at home . . . one Thursday morning, when we had been married about eight months. . . . On the Friday, as I was at work as usual with the boats, I heard a noise behind me, on the road which ran by the side of the canal: I turned to look, and saw a gang of slaves coming. When they came up to me, one of them cried out, "Moses, my dear!" I wondered who among them should know me, and found it was my wife. She cried out to me, "I am gone." I was struck with consternation. Mr. Rogerson was with them, on his horse, armed with pistols. I said to him, "for God's sake, have you bought my wife?" He said he had; when I asked him what she had done; he said she had done nothing, but that her master wanted money.

He drew out a pistol, and said that if I went near the waggon on which she was, he would shoot me. I asked for leave to shake hands with her, which he refused, but said I might stand at a distance and talk with her. My heart was so full, that I could say very little. I asked leave to give her a dram [money]: he told Mr. Burgess, the man who was with him, to get down and carry it to her. I gave her the little money I had in my pocket, and bid her farewell. I have never seen or heard of her from that day to this. I loved her as I loved my life.

—*From* Narrative of the Life of Moses Grandy; Late a Slave in the United States of America. *London: C. Gilpin, 1843. Available online at: http://docsouth.unc.edu/grandy/grandy.html*

Andrew Goodman: "The Bestest Man God Made in a Long Time"

More often than not, the slave narratives tell difficult and complex stories, stories of the tired, overworked, abused, and grieving, of slave owners who were heartless at best, cruel or even murderous at worst. Another kind of narrative exists, however, one that offers a glimpse of humanity in this dark period of American history. In the following passage, from the narrative of Andrew Goodman of Texas, you'll hear a different tale—about the kindness of one owner and the people whose lives he made better.

"I never was cold and hungry."

I WAS BORN IN SLAVERY and I think them days was better for the niggers than the days we see now. One thing was, I never was cold and hungry when my old master lived, and I has been plenty hungry and cold a lot of times since he is gone. But sometimes I think Marse Goodman was the bestest man God made in a long time.

. . . Old Marse never 'lowed none of his nigger families separated. . . .

he thought it right and fittin' that folks stay together, though I heard tell of some that didn't think so.

My Missus [the master's wife] was just as good as Marse Bob. My maw was a puny little woman that wasn't able to do work in the fields, and she puttered round the house for the Missus, doin' little odd jobs. I played round with little Miss Sallie and little Mr. Bob [the master's children], and I ate with them and slept with them. I used to sweep off the steps and do things, and she'd brag on me. Many is the time I'd get to noddin' and go to sleep, and she'd pick me up and put me in bed with her chillen.

Marse Bob didn't put his little niggers in the fields till they's big 'nough to work. . . . He didn't never put the niggers out in bad weather. He give us something to do, in out of the weather, like shellin' corn, and the women could spin and knit. . . .

Some owners treated their slaves with kindness and decency. They might even continue to take an interest in the welfare of former slaves after emancipation, as shown here in *A Visit from the Old Mistress*, painted by famous American artist Winslow Homer in 1876.

. . . We raised cotton and grain and chickens and vegetables, and most anything anybody could ask for.

Some places the masters give out a peck of meal and so many pounds of meat to a family for them a week's rations, and if they ate it up that was all they got. But Marse Bob always give out plenty, and said, "If you need more you can have it, 'cause ain't any going to suffer on my place."

He built us a church, and a old man, Kenneth Lyons, who was a slave of the Lyons' family nearby, used to get a pass every Sunday mornin' and come preach to us. He was a man of good learnin' and the best preacher I ever heard. . . . Then on Sunday afternoon, Marse Bob learned us to read and write. He told us we oughta get all the learnin' we could.

Once a week the slaves could have any night they want for a dance or frolic. . . . Marse Bob give us chickens or kilt a fresh beef or let us make 'lasses [molasses] candy. We could choose any night, 'cept in the fall of the year. Then we worked awful hard and didn't have the time. . . . Marse always give us from Christmas Eve through New Year's Day off, to make up for the hard work in the fall.

. . . Course, we used to hear about other places where they had nigger drivers and beat the slaves. But I never did see or hear tell of one of master's slaves gittin' a beatin'. . . . Marse Bob never had no niggers to run off.

—From Norman R. Yetman, editor. Voice from Slavery: 100 Authentic Slave Narratives *[narratives from the Federal Writer's Project interviews]. Minneola, NY: Dover, 2000. Original work published 1972.*

Think about This

1. Why had Goodman's life been better in slavery than it was after gaining his freedom?
2. List several ways that Andrew's experience was different from those of many other slaves, including those described in the narratives you have read here.

Chapter 4

Slave Narratives: Women Tell Their Stories

THE THOUSANDS OF NARRATIVES available to us today provide a view of slavery from many diverse perspectives. Among the most interesting viewpoints are those of African-American women. In an age when few women, regardless of their race, had their voices heard, black women—slaves and former slaves—were publishing autobiographies, and interviewers were listening as intently to their life stories as to those of their male counterparts. For this reason, we have a fascinating picture of what it was like to be a woman, and a slave, in nineteenth-century America.

Elizabeth Keckley: "Sold, Like the Hogs"

Elizabeth Hobbs Keckley was born into slavery in 1818. By 1855 she had saved enough money to buy her freedom. She eventually worked at the White House as a dressmaker for Mary Todd Lincoln. At age fifty she published her autobiography, *Behind the Scenes, Or, Thirty Years a Slave and Four Years in the White House,* portions of which are reprinted here. In this selection, Elizabeth

Women seem to find comfort in each other's presence as they wait to be sold at a Virginia slave market.

recounts her childhood memory of a young boy who was separated from his family and sold.

WHEN I WAS ABOUT SEVEN YEARS OLD I witnessed, for the first time, the sale of a human being. We were living at Prince Edward, in Virginia, and master had just purchased his hogs for the winter, for which he was unable to pay in full. To escape from his embarrassment it was necessary to sell one of the slaves. Little Joe, the son of the cook, was selected as the victim. His mother was ordered to dress him up in his Sunday clothes, and send him to the house. He came in with a bright face, was placed in the scales, and was sold, like the hogs, at so much per pound. His mother was kept in ignorance of the transaction, but her suspicions were aroused. When her son started for Petersburgh in the wagon, the truth began to dawn upon her mind, and she pleaded piteously that her boy should not be taken from her; but master quieted her by telling her that he was simply going to town with the wagon, and would be back in the morning.

". . . she was whipped for grieving for her lost boy."

Morning came, but little Joe did not return to his mother. Morning after morning passed, and the mother went down to the grave without ever seeing her child again. One day she was whipped for grieving for her lost boy. Colonel Burwell never liked to see one of his slaves wear a sorrowful face, and those who offended in this particular way were always punished. Alas! the sunny face of the slave is not always an indication of sunshine in the heart.

—*From Elizabeth Keckley,* Behind the Scenes, Or, Thirty Years a Slave and Four Years in the White House. *Schomburg Library of Nineteenth-Century Black Women Writers. New York: Oxford University Press, 1989.*

Think about This

Why didn't the master tell Little Joe's mother what he planned to do? Why do you think she was suspicious?

Elizabeth Keckley: "I Will Know Why I Have Been Flogged"

Cruel punishment was not reserved solely for male slaves; women too faced the lash and other harsh forms of reprimand. In the following passage, Elizabeth Keckley recalls being whipped by her master's friend, at whose home she had been working.

MR. BINGHAM [THE MASTER'S FRIEND] CAME TO THE DOOR and asked me to go with him to his study. Wondering what he meant by his strange request, I followed him, and when we had entered the study he closed the door, and in his blunt way remarked: "Lizzie, I am going to flog you." I was thunderstruck, and tried to think if I had been remiss in anything. I could not recollect of doing anything to deserve punishment, and with surprise exclaimed: "Whip me, Mr. Bingham! what for?"

"No matter," he replied, "I am going to whip you, so take down your dress this instant."

Recollect, I was eighteen years of age, was a woman fully developed, and yet this man coolly bade me take down my dress. I drew myself up proudly, firmly, and said: "No, Mr. Bingham, I shall not take down my dress before you. Moreover, you shall not whip me unless you prove the stronger. Nobody has a right to whip me but my own master, and nobody shall do so if I can prevent it."

"Whip me, Mr. Bingham! what for?"

My words seemed to exasperate him. He seized a rope, caught me roughly, and tried to tie me. I resisted with all my strength, but he was the stronger of the two, and after a hard struggle succeeded in binding my hands and tearing my dress from my back. Then he picked up a rawhide, and began to ply it freely over my shoulders. With steady hand and practised eye he would raise the instrument of torture, nerve himself for a blow, and with fearful force the rawhide descended upon the quivering flesh. It cut the skin, raised great welts, and the warm blood trickled down my back. Oh God! I can feel the torture now—the terrible, excruciating agony of those moments. I did not scream; I was too proud to let my tormentor know what I was suffering. . . .

As soon as I was released, stunned with pain, bruised and bleeding, I went home and rushed into the presence of the pastor and his wife [her master and mistress], wildly exclaiming: "Master Robert, why did you let Mr. Bingham flog me? What have I done that I should be so punished?"

This scene may be melodramatic, but it does illustrate the fact that in the slavery system, women were just as capable of cruelty as men. Female slaves might be punished by their mistresses as well as by their masters.

"Go away," he gruffly answered, "do not bother me."

I would not be put off thus. "What have I done? I will know why I have been flogged."

I saw his cheeks flush with anger, but I did not move. He rose to his feet, and on my refusing to go without an explanation, seized a chair, struck me, and felled me to the floor. I rose, bewildered, almost dead with pain, crept to my room, dressed my bruised arms and back as best I could, and then lay down, but not to sleep. No, I could not sleep, for I was suffering mental as well as bodily torture. My spirit rebelled against the unjustness that had been inflicted upon me, and though I tried to smother my anger and to forgive those who had been so cruel to me, it was impossible. It seems that Mr. Bingham had pledged himself to Mrs. Burwell [Elizabeth's mistress] to subdue what he called my "stubborn pride."

—From Elizabeth Keckley, Behind the Scenes, Or, Thirty Years a Slave and Four Years in the White House. *Schomburg Library of Nineteenth-Century Black Women Writers. New York: Oxford University Press, 1989.*

Think about This

1. The physical pain of this punishment was hard to bear, but what other aspects of Elizabeth's experience made the situation even worse?
2. What was Elizabeth's master's occupation? Should this have had some effect on his treatment of her?

Harriet Jacobs: "I Was His Property"

"I was so fondly shielded," Harriet Jacobs wrote of her childhood, "that I never dreamed I was a piece of merchandise." Harriet lived in a comfortable house with her brother and parents, both of whom were children of white fathers and black mothers. When her mother died, six-year-old Harriet learned "by the talk around me, that I was a slave." In the following passage, Harriet describes turning fifteen years old. She was a beautiful girl, and her master—forty years her senior—began to take a sexual interest in her. Harriet took drastic measures to avoid his pursuit, but he made her life extremely difficult. Unfortunately, what Harriet describes was all too common an experience for slave women.

import
meaning

I NOW ENTERED ON MY FIFTEENTH YEAR—a sad epoch in the life of a slave girl. My master began to whisper foul words in my ear. Young as I was, I could not remain ignorant of their import. . . . He peopled my young mind with unclean images, such as only a vile monster could think of. I turned from him with disgust and hatred. But he was my master. I was compelled to live under the same roof with him. . . . He told me I was his property; that I must be subject to his will in all things. My soul revolted against the mean tyranny. But where could I turn for protection? . . .

"But where could I turn for protection?"

[In the life of a slave girl] there is no shadow of law to protect her from insult, from violence, or even from death; all these are inflicted by fiends who bear the shape of men. The mistress, who ought to protect the helpless victim, has no other feelings towards her but those of jealousy and rage. . . .

Even the little child, who is accustomed to wait on her mistress and her children, will learn, before she is twelve years old, why it is

A slave auction in the 1850s. The woman in the center will probably sell for a high price because of her beauty, but will almost certainly suffer unwanted attention from her master.

that her mistress hates such and such a one among the slaves. . . . She listens to violent outbreaks of jealous passion, and cannot help understanding what is the cause. She will become prematurely knowing in evil things. Soon she will learn to tremble when she hears her master's footfall. She will be compelled to realize that she is no longer a child. If God has bestowed beauty upon her, it will prove her greatest curse. That which commands admiration in the white woman only hastens the degradation of the female slave. . . .

I longed for some one to confide in. . . . But Dr. Flint [Harriet's master] swore he would kill me, if I was not as silent as the grave. Then, although my grandmother was all in all to me, I feared her as well as loved her. . . . I was very young, and felt shamefaced about telling her such impure things. . . .

—*From Harriet Jacobs,* Incidents in the Life of a Slave Girl. *In* The Classic Slave Narratives, *edited by Henry Louis Gates, Jr. New York: Signet Classic, 2002. Original work published in 1861.*

Think about This

1. Harriet offers explanations for why she could not tell anyone about what was happening to her. What were they?
2. According to Harriet, who might be expected to protect a slave girl from a master's sexual advances? Why wouldn't this person help her?
3. In your own words, explain the following sentence: "That which commands admiration in the white woman only hastens the degradation of the female slave."

Charlotte Brooks: "I Finally Got Religion"

For many American slaves, religion provided a refuge. In the colonial years, new arrivals from Africa often continued to practice the religions of their homeland, but as time passed, generations born in the New World were increasingly drawn to the faith practiced all around them: Christianity. Sometimes they went to their masters' churches, sitting in a special area reserved for slaves. Other times a preacher visited slaves in their quarters. Often slaves received little religious instruction beyond admonitions to obey their masters. In one narrative, former slave Lucretia Alexander described the religious service of one preacher as follows: "He'd just say, 'Serve your masters. Don't steal your master's turkey. Don't steal your master's chickens. Don't steal your master's hogs. Don't steal your master's meat. Do whatsomeever your master tell you to do.' Same old thing all de time."

Perhaps most important to African Americans were the communities of faith that grew and flourished within their own world, with their friends and families. In their quarters, slaves held secret prayer meetings, risking severe punishment for doing so. There they listened to black preachers, who often took great risks themselves by sneaking out of their plantations to spread the word of God. Following is one woman's recollection of the importance of religion in her life.

I FINALLY GOT RELIGION, and it was Aunt Jane's praying and singing them old Virginia hymns that helped me so much. Aunt Jane's marster would let her come to see me sometimes, but not often. Sometimes she would slip away from her place at night and come to see me anyhow. She would hold prayer-meeting in my house whenever she would come to see me. . . .

. . . if old marster heard us singing and praying he would come out and make us stop. One time, I remember, we all were having a prayer-meeting in my cabin, and marster came up to the door and hollered out, "You, Charlotte, what's all that fuss in there?" We all had to hush up for that night. I was so afraid old marster would see Aunt Jane. I knew Aunt Jane would have to suffer if her white people knew she was off at night. Marster used to say God was tired of us all hollering to him at night.

. . . none of us listened to him about singing and praying. I tell you we used to have some good times together praying and singing.

Faith and prayer helped African Americans through hard times both during and after slavery. This 1894 painting is by African-American artist Henry Ossawa Tanner, one of the first American painters to portray black subjects with realism and dignity.

He did not want us to pray, but we would have our little prayer-meeting anyhow. Sometimes when we met to hold our meetings we would put a big wash-tub full of water in the middle of the floor to catch the sound of our voices when we sung. When we all sung we would march around and shake each other's hands, and we would sing easy and low, so marster could not hear us. O, how happy I used to be in those meetings, although I was a slave!

—From Octavia V. Rogers, The House of Bondage, or, Charlotte Brooks and Other Slaves, Original and Life Like. *New York: Hunt & Eaton, 1890. Available online at: http://docsouth.unc.edu/neh/albert/albert.html#albert11*

Think about This

1. Why do you think masters tried to prevent slaves from meeting?

2. In what ways do you think religion may have been important to slaves?

Tempe Herndon Durham: "We Had a Big Weddin'"

If religion provided one source of solace for slaves, family provided another. Slaves could not legally marry, but this did not keep them from holding wedding ceremonies, and it certainly did not prevent them from forming strong lifelong unions—if they had the good fortune not to be separated. The threat of separation was always very real. Also, many husbands and wives were unable to live together. Against these odds, couples worked to forge bonds that would offer them the peace and comfort of a family. And sometimes they were supported by their owners. Tempe Herndon Durham grew up on a large plantation in North Carolina, owned by George and Betsy Herndon. Tempe married Exter Durham on the front porch of the Herndons' home, and the Herndons held a lively celebration in the couple's honor. In the following narrative, she describes the happy day.

WE HAD A BIG WEDDIN'. We was married on de front po'ch of de big house. Marse George killed a shoat an' Mis' Betsy had Georgianna, de cook, to bake a big weddin' cake all iced up white as snow wid a bride an' groom standin' in de middle holdin' han's. De table was set out in de yard under de trees, an' you ain't never seed de like of eats. All de niggers come to de feas'. . . . Dat was some weddin'. I had on a white dress, white shoes an' long white gloves dat come to my elbow, an' Mis' Betsy done made me a weddin' veil out of a white net window curtain. When she played de weddin' ma'ch on de piano, me an' Exter ma'ched down de walk an' up on de po'ch to de altar Mis' Betsy done

shoat
young hog

"Dat was some weddin'."

fixed. Dat de pretties' altar I ever seed. Back 'gainst de rose vine dat was full of red roses, Mis' Betsy done put tables filled wid flowers an' white candles. . . . Exter done made me a weddin' ring. He made it out of a big red button wid his pocket knife. He done cut it so roun' an' polished it so smooth dat it looked like a red satin ribbon tide 'roun' my finger. Dat sho was a pretty ring. I wore it 'bout fifty years, den it got so thin dat I lost it one day in de wash tub when I was washin' clothes.

Uncle Edmond Kirby married us. He was de nigger preacher dat preached at de plantation church. After Uncle Edmond said de las' words over me an' Exter, Marse George got to have his little fun: He say, "Come on, Exter, you an' Tempie got to jump over de broom stick backwards; you got to do dat to see which one gwine be boss of your househol'." Everybody come stan' 'roun to watch. Marse George hold de broom 'bout a foot high off de floor. De one dat jump over

Folk art often depicts people and scenes ignored by formal art. Here, slaves in Lynchburg, Virginia, enjoy a dance in 1853.

it backwards an' never touch de handle, gwine boss de house, an' if bof [both] of dem jump over widout touchin' it, [there won't] be no bossin', dey jus' . . . be 'genial. I jumped fus', an' you ought to seed me. I sailed right over dat broom stick same as a cricket, but when Exter jump . . . his feets was so big an' clumsy dat dey got all tangled up in dat broom an' he fell head long. Marse George he laugh an' laugh, an' tole Exter he [was going to] be bossed 'twell [till] he skeered to speak less'n I tole him to speak. After de weddin' we went down to de cabin Mis' Betsy done all dressed up, but Exter couldn' stay no longer den dat night kaze he belonged to Marse Snipes Durham an' he had to go back home. He lef' de nex day for his plantation, but he come back every Saturday night an' stay 'twell Sunday night. We had eleven chillun. Nine was bawn befo' surrender an' two after we was set free. So I had two chillun dat wuzn' bawn in bondage. I was worth a heap to Marse George kaze I had so many chillun. De more chillun a slave had de more dey was worth. Lucy Carter was de only nigger on de plantation dat had more chillun den I had. She had twelve, but her chillun was sickly an' mine was muley strong an' healthy. Dey never was sick.

'genial
friendly

—From the narrative of Tempe Herndon Durham. Available online at American Slave Narratives: An Online Anthology. *http://xroads.virginia.edu/~hyper/wpa/index.html*

Think about This

1. Tempe describes a wedding tradition known as "jumping the broom." From what she said, what is the significance of this activity?
2. Why do you think the Herndons allowed Tempe to marry Exter? What impression do you have of the Herndons after reading her description of them?
3. Tempe says she was "worth a heap" to George Herndon. What does she mean by this?

For slave families, escape was often the only hope of staying together. *A Ride for Liberty—The Fugitive Slaves* was painted by noted American artist Eastman Johnson in 1862.

Chapter 5

Escape and Revolt

DESPITE THE COMFORTS of family and religion, African Americans yearned to be free. There were many ways they tried to break slavery's bonds. Some attempted to revolt, hoping to rally a sufficient force of rebels to overwhelm their masters. But these relatively rare attempts at insurrection always failed. Slaves usually chose to fight smaller battles instead. Some resisted by pretending to be sick or to misunderstand instructions. Others resorted to theft, arson, or even murder. In a few extreme cases, parents, rather than see their children grow up in bondage, were driven to kill them. This also deprived their masters of valuable property.

The majority of those who fought slavery did so by attempting escape. No one knows for sure how many actually managed to reach freedom, but estimates suggest the number to be about one thousand per year. Some slaves did not run away permanently, but left to visit spouses or children or to avoid sale or punishment. Sometimes groups of slaves ran away together to protest excessive work or mistreatment.

For three decades before the Civil War, abolitionists worked to build secret networks to assist runaway slaves, the most famous of which was the Underground Railroad. Such networks, led by courageous abolitionists such as Harriet Tubman and Levi Coffin, did help some men and women reach freedom in the North, but most runaways had only themselves to rely on. Some fled to freedom using forged or borrowed passes. Others stowed away on boats or trains. A few escapees created ingenious disguises for themselves. For many runaways, however, reaching Northern cities was impossible. Instead, they hid in Southern cities and swamps. Some concealed themselves in forests near their owners' homes until they were captured, or until they had no choice but to return on their own.

For every successful escape, many more failed. Slave owners often reserved the most brutal treatment for runaways. "Nothing seems to give the slaveholders so much pleasure as the catching and torturing of fugitives," recalled William Craft, whose story is included in this chapter. To track down and capture their slaves, owners often resorted to the professional services of slave hunters. "The slaveholders and their hired ruffians," recalled Craft, "appear to take more pleasure in this inhuman pursuit than English sportsmen do in chasing a fox or a stag."

The following passages tell various tales of escape and revolt: some successful, others not. In each passage, however, you will witness passionate emotions—love, hate, courage—and sometimes violence. These are stories of a people struggling to be free.

The Turner Rebellion

Nat Turner led the largest and most devastating slave revolt in U.S. history. Turner was born a slave on a plantation in

Southampton County, Virginia, in 1800. His parents and grandmother encouraged him to get an education and resist slavery. Turner was sold several times. A son of one of his masters taught him to read and write, and he eventually became a preacher. His master at the time permitted him to travel to various plantations in the county to spread the word of God. Turner believed himself to be a prophet, "ordained for some great purpose, in the hands of the Almighty." That purpose, he thought, was to end slavery through violent revolt, and he spread his message from meeting house to meeting house.

Nat Turner making plans with his fellow rebels, as imagined by a nineteenth-century artist.

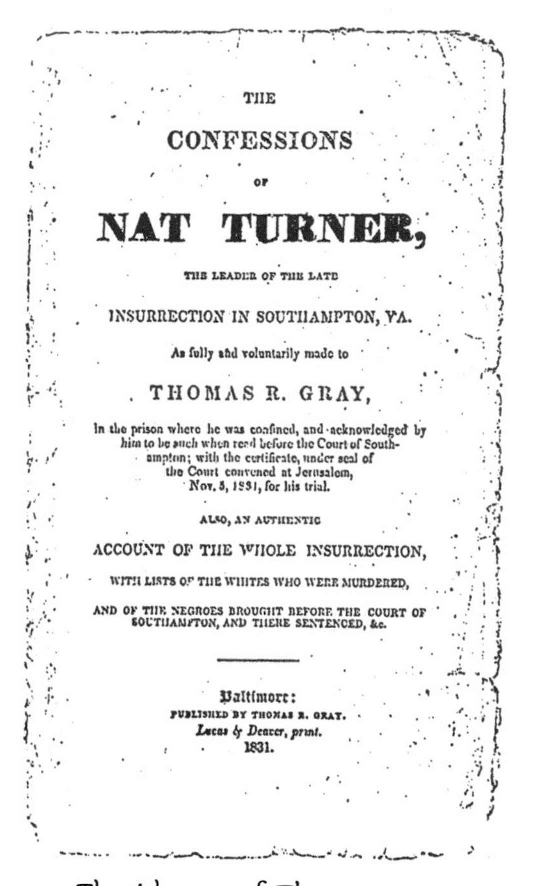
THE

CONFESSIONS

OF

NAT TURNER,

THE LEADER OF THE LATE

INSURRECTION IN SOUTHAMPTON, VA.

As fully and voluntarily made to

THOMAS R. GRAY,

In the prison where he was confined, and acknowledged by him to be such when read before the Court of Southampton; with the certificate, under seal of the Court convened at Jerusalem, Nov. 5, 1831, for his trial.

ALSO, AN AUTHENTIC

ACCOUNT OF THE WHOLE INSURRECTION,

WITH LISTS OF THE WHITES WHO WERE MURDERED,

AND OF THE NEGROES BROUGHT BEFORE THE COURT OF SOUTHAMPTON, AND THERE SENTENCED, &c.

Baltimore:
PUBLISHED BY THOMAS R. GRAY.
Lucas & Deaver, print.
1831.

The title page of *The Confessions of Nat Turner* notes that Turner acknowledged before the court trying him that he had made this account of his rebellion "fully and voluntarily."

The revolt began on August 22, 1831, when Turner and four other slaves attacked the family of Turner's owner, killing everyone in the household, including an infant. In the following days, the band moved from house to house, killing any white person the group encountered—including women and children. At each house, more slaves joined Turner's band. The three-day rebellion ended in the deaths of more than fifty white people. Authorities killed about one hundred African Americans; twenty more were later executed for their involvement. Turner eluded capture for two months. When he was taken in, he told his story to an attorney, Thomas Gray, who published it as *The Confessions of Nat Turner.* Turner was hanged less than two weeks later. Following is a passage from the *Confessions.*

'TWAS MY OBJECT TO CARRY TERROR AND DEVASTATION wherever we went. . . . I sometimes got in sight in time to see the work of death completed, viewed the mangled bodies as they lay, in silent satisfaction, and immediately started in quest of other victims—Having murdered Mrs. Waller and ten children, we started for Mr. William Williams'—having killed him and two little boys that were there; while engaged in this, Mrs. Williams fled and got some distance from the house, but she was pursued, overtaken, and compelled to get up behind one of the company, who brought her back, and after showing her the mangled body of her lifeless husband, she was told to get down and lay by his side, where she was shot dead. . . .

Our number amounted now to fifty or sixty, all mounted and armed with guns, axes, swords, and clubs. . . . We were met by a party of white men, who had pursued our blood-stained track. . . . The white men, eighteen in number, approached us in about one hundred yards, when one of them fired. . . . I then ordered my men to fire and rush them; the few remaining stood their ground until we approached within fifty yards, when they fired and retreated. . . . As I saw them re-loading their guns, and more coming up than I saw at first, and several of my bravest men being wounded, the other became panick struck and squandered over the field; the white men pursued and fired on us several times. . . .

"I then ordered my men to fire and rush them."

—*From* The Confessions of Nat Turner, the Leader of the Late Insurrection in South Hampton, VA. *Baltimore: Lucas & Deaver, 1831.*

Think about This

1. Did Nat Turner appear to show any remorse in his confession? Do you think his actions were justified?
2. Nat Turner believed that God had told him to rebel. Can you think of other cases in which people have used religion to defend their actions?

Virginia Laws Curtail Slaves' Religious Gatherings

Shortly after the Turner rebellion, the Virginia state government enacted laws to try to prevent a similar event from happening again. In the following passage, a former slave named Cyrus Branch explains the effects of this legislation. Vermont writer Elizabeth Merwin Wickham interviewed Branch when he was reunited

In Virginia, prayer meetings like this one had to be held in secret after the Turner rebellion.

with his family following decades of separation. His story, including this excerpt, was published in the *Manchester Journal* (Vermont) in January 1869.

THE STATE GOVERNMENT SOON AFTER [the Turner rebellion] enacted a law prohibiting colored men entirely from preaching and exhorting, or even gathering for prayer meetings, except at the leaves of their respective owners. These were hard laws to submit to, their situation as slaves being made bearable to some only by the soothing counsels and influence of their christian brethren. But the moral courage of a few of the preachers rose superior to the laws of the land, when they were in violation of the laws of God as revealed in the Scriptures. Among such men was one Pleasant Randall, the property of Mr. Harrison, of Charles City, who deemed his commission to make the Gospel known to sinners, to be from the Lord, and not from man.

". . . the moral courage of a few of the preachers rose superior to the laws of the land."

When gone into Prince George County, one Saturday, to preach for a couple of days, the planters in the vicinity visited his master, Mr. Harrison, urging him to restrain Randall, or shut him up, saying, that his preaching so affected their people that they would bear beating and beating, and then hear him again at the first opportunity—they could not thus spare their time, and the man ought, by the laws, to be hung—and they should do something to stop him, if he did not. Mr. Harrison was personally attached to the good man, and told them, that no mob should touch him; they must proceed according to law if they meant to hinder his preaching. So Randall was arrested, imprisoned, and tried, and convicted, and condemned to be hung, for making eternal salvation known to his fellows, and an early day was fixed for his execution.

—From E. M. W. (Elizabeth Merwin Wickham), A Lost Family Found; An Authentic Narrative of Cyrus Branch and His Family, Alias John White of Manchester, Vermont, *1869. Available online at: http://docsouth.unc.edu/neh/wickham/menu.html*

Think about This

1. Pleasant Randall was clearly a charismatic preacher if the slaves would bear beating after beating in order to listen to him. According to Cyrus Branch, Randall's main concern was for the salvation of the slaves' souls. Why then would the planters want him stopped?
2. Think about what the First Amendment—part of the Bill of Rights—says about freedom of religion. Was it acceptable to arrest, try, and sentence Pleasant Randall to death?
3. Pleasant Randall believed that he was following a higher authority than the Virginia state legislature. So did Nat Turner. In each case, the individual was following "the will of God." In judging them, how does one differentiate between a truly moral person and a fanatic?

A Family Poisoned

In the following newspaper account, a reporter describes the case of a family poisoned by their slave—a girl of ten or twelve.

A Family Poisoned by a Slave Child only Twelve Years Old.

From the Louisville Courier, July 13.

Great excitement was created yesterday by the report that poison had been administered to the family of Mrs. Patrick H. Pope. . . . The persons affected were Mrs. Pope, her daughter ELLA, MISS GREEN, of Danville, Ky., and a negro servant. The poison was arsenic, which was put into the coffee-pot while it was on the table, as confessed by the slave girl, CHARITY, who is ten or twelve years of age. Those of the family we name, shortly after breakfast were affected with vomiting, thirst, and other indications that they had swallowed poison. Antidotes were promptly administered, and last evening, we are happy to say, all were out of danger. . . .

The poison was obtained from the drug store of W. H. YOUNG. . . . The girl CHARITY, in the absence of the proprietor, early in the morning applied to the attendant, a boy of 14 years, for arsenic, and said her mistress wanted to kill rats. The boy refused, saying MR. YOUNG had given strict orders to let no servant or minor have arsenic without an order. He told her to get it from her mistress. She went out, and in a few minutes returned, saying her mistress said she hadn't time to write it then, but to send it. As the lady often got articles, and deceived by the plausibility of the precocious girl, he gave the arsenic. This, as mentioned, she confesses to placing in the coffee.

"The poison was arsenic."

Here is the story of the girl as related to Policeman CARTER TILLER, who arrested her: "I told a yellow man [mulatto?], named Jerry, that I had been mistreated by the family, he said poison them . . . he intended to do the same thing when his mistress' family came home; he told me to put it in the coffee pot, and that would kill them. I put it in before they came to breakfast; he said as soon as I saw them crying and vomiting I must run away. As soon as they commenced vomiting I went to the back gate and took to my heels and ran away. I don't know where I was going."

TILLER caught her a mile from the city.

—From the Louisville Courier. *Reprinted in* Lest We Forget *by Velma Maia Thomas. New York: Crown, 1997.*

Henry "Box" Brown: A Daring Escape

Although Henry Brown would later describe his life in slavery as "tolerable," one event drove him to attempt escape: the sale of his wife and three children. Knowing the dangers a runaway faced, Brown devised an ingenious plan. William Still of Philadelphia wrote the following account of his story. Still, a freeborn black man, helped many fugitives find their way to freedom. He wrote the first detailed record of the Underground Railroad, of which Brown's story is a part. Still's work remains an important contribution to the study of slavery.

BROWN COUNTED WELL THE COST before venturing upon his hazardous undertaking. Ordinary modes of travel he concluded might prove disastrous to his hopes; he, therefore, hit upon a new invention altogether, which was to have himself boxed up and forwarded to Philadelphia direct by express. The size of the box and how it was to be made to fit him most comfortably, was of his own ordering. Two feet eight inches deep, two feet wide, and three feet long were the exact dimensions of the box, lined with baize. His resources in regard to food and water consisted of the following: One bladder of water and a few small biscuits. His mechanical implement to meet the death-struggle for fresh air, all told, was one large gimlet. Satisfied that it would be far better to peril his life for freedom in this way than to remain under the galling yoke of Slavery, he entered his box, which was safely nailed up and hooped with five hickory hoops, and then was addressed by his . . . friend, James A. Smith, a shoe dealer, to Wm. H. Johnson, Arch Street, Philadelphia, marked, "This side up with

"This side up with care."

baize *coarse fabric*

gimlet *a tool to drill holes*

care." . . . It was twenty-six hours from the time he left Richmond until his arrival in the city of Brotherly Love. The notice, "This side up, etc.," did not avail with the different expressmen, who hesitated not to handle the box in the usual rough manner. . . . For a while they actually had the box upside down, and had him on his head for miles.

Henry "Box" Brown arrives in Philadelphia, completing his bold and unconventional escape from slavery. Frederick Douglass (*second from left*) assists in lifting off the box lid.

[Brown arrives at his destination.]

The witnesses will never forget that moment. Saw and hatchet quickly had the five hickory hoops cut and the lid off, and the marvelous resurrection of Brown ensued. Rising up in the box, he reached out his hand, saying, "How do you do, gentlemen?" The little assemblage hardly knew what to think or do at the moment.

—*From William Still,* Still's Underground Railroad Records. *Revised edition. Philadelphia: William Still (publisher), 1883.*

Ellen and William Craft: A Cunning Plan

In December 1848 William and Ellen Craft, husband and wife, contrived a brilliant plan of escape, one that would allow them to take public transportation out of Georgia, all the way to Philadelphia, staying in fine hotels along the way. It worked, and after their arrival in the City of Brotherly Love, they made their way to Boston. But their masters eventually discovered where they were and sent slave hunters to bring them back. The Crafts were determined not to return to a life of bondage. With the help of abolitionists, they moved to England, where slavery was illegal. After the Civil War the couple returned to the United States, bought a farm, and opened a school for black children. Following is William's account of their extraordinary plan.

KNOWING THAT SLAVEHOLDERS HAVE the privilege of taking their slaves to any part of the country they think proper, it occurred to me that, as my wife was nearly white, I might get her to disguise herself as an invalid gentleman, and assume to be my master, while I could attend as his slave, and that in this manner we might effect our escape. . . .

. . . I went to different parts of the town, at odd times, and purchased things piece by piece . . . and took them home to the house where my wife resided. . . . when we fancied we had everything ready the time was fixed for the flight. But we knew it would not do to start off without first getting our masters' consent to be away for a few days. Had we left without this, they would soon have had us back into slavery, and probably we should never have got another fair opportunity of even attempting to escape.

Ellen Craft, in her disguise as an invalid white gentleman

Some of the best slave-holders will sometimes give their favourite slaves a few days' holiday at Christmas time; so, after no little amount of perseverance on my wife's part, she obtained a pass from her mistress, allowing her to be away for a few days. The cabinet-maker with whom I worked gave me a similar paper. . . .

. . . when the thought flashed across my wife's mind, that it was customary for travellers to register their names in the visitors' book at hotels, as well as in the clearance or Custom-house book at Charleston, South Carolina—it made our spirits droop within us.

So, while sitting in our little room upon the verge of despair, all at once my wife raised her head, and with a smile upon her face, which was a moment before bathed in tears, said, "I think I have it! . . . I think I can make a poultice and bind up my right hand in a sling, and with propriety ask the officers to register my name for me. . . ."

It then occurred to her that the smoothness of her face might betray her; so she decided to make another poultice, and put it in a white handkerchief to be worn under the chin, up the cheeks, and to tie over the head. This nearly hid the expression of the countenance, as well as the beardless chin. . . .

poultice
dressing for an injury

William Craft, whose ingenious plan won his and his wife's freedom

We sat up all night discussing the plan, and making preparations. Just before the time arrived, in the morning, for us to leave, I cut off my wife's hair square at the back of the head, and got her to dress in the disguise and stand out on the floor. I found that she made a most respectable looking gentleman.

—From William Craft, Running a Thousand Miles for Freedom. *London: William Twedie, 1860. Available online at Electronic Text Center, University of Virginia Library: http://etext.lib.virginia.edu/toc/modeng/public/CraThou.html*

Think about This

1. Briefly describe the Crafts' plan for escape. What characteristic of Ellen's made it possible?
2. Why were the Crafts worried about the fact that travelers had to register their names at hotels and the customhouse?
3. Why do you think the Crafts did not try to escape with Ellen acting as a free white woman and William as her slave?

Chapter 6

Abolitionists and the March toward War

IN THE HALF CENTURY LEADING up to the Civil War, conflict intensified between pro- and antislavery forces. By the 1830s, abolitionists had begun to gain political power, and the nation's future grew ever more uncertain. The cry to end slavery across the land no longer came from a tiny minority. In this tense atmosphere, the turbulent theme of slavery found its way to the very core of political power—Capitol Hill.

In an attempt to calm each side of the issue, Congress passed a series of laws known as the Compromise of 1850. The compromise gave both sides part of what they wanted. One law meant to pacify abolitionists ensured that slavery would be prohibited in California, for example. Likewise the Fugitive Slave Act was intended to satisfy the slave owners. According to this law, a person suspected of being a runaway could be arrested and turned over to anyone who claimed to own him or her—with nothing more than the claimant's sworn testimony of ownership. Suspected runaways did not have the right to a trial by jury, nor could they

John Brown, one of the most ardent and radical of the abolitionists. This photograph was taken about three years before the insurrection he led in 1859, which probably hastened the march toward the Civil War.

testify on their own behalf. Any person who helped a runaway by providing shelter, food, or any other form of assistance was liable to be punished by six months in prison and a $1,000 fine. Because bounty hunters and others who captured fugitives received a reward, the act also encouraged some to kidnap free blacks and sell them to slave owners.

Ironically, the results of the Fugitive Slave Act would be exactly the opposite of what its framers intended. Abolitionists despised the new law. In fact, rather than deterring them from helping runaways, it galvanized their efforts and helped push the country closer to civil war. Fifteen years after the passage of the act, slavery would be history. This chapter features the words of some of the most well-known abolitionists.

William Lloyd Garrison: "I Will Be Heard!"

Many early abolitionists believed the process of emancipation should be gradual, but as time went by this attitude changed, in part because of the work of William Lloyd Garrison. An outspoken critic of slavery, Garrison started an antislavery paper, *The Liberator,* in 1831. For thirty-five years, the paper attacked not only slaveholders, but also those abolitionists who were opposed to rapid, unequivocal change. Some people considered Garrison's position too radical, but it opened the eyes of many. Following is a portion of his editorial, "To the Public," published in the first issue of *The Liberator.*

I SHALL STRENUOUSLY CONTEND for the immediate enfranchisement of our slave population. [O]n the Fourth of July, 1829, in an address on slavery, I unreflectingly assented to the popular but pernicious doctrine of gradual abolition. I seize this opportunity to make a full and unequivocal recantation, and thus publicly to ask pardon of my God, of my country, and of my brethren the poor slaves, for having uttered a sentiment so full of timidity, injustice and absurdity. . . .

I am aware, that many object to the severity of my language; but is there not cause for severity? I will be as harsh as truth, and as uncompromising as justice. On this subject, I do not wish to think, or speak, or write, with moderation. No! no! Tell a man whose house is on fire, to give a moderate alarm; . . . tell the mother to gradually extricate her babe from the

William Lloyd Garrison (1805–1879). The masthead of his influential newspaper, *The Liberator*, states the humanitarian principles that led him to oppose slavery.

THE LIBERATOR.

VOL. I.] WILLIAM LLOYD GARRISON AND ISAAC KNAPP, PUBLISHERS. [NO. 22

BOSTON, MASSACHUSETTS.] OUR COUNTRY IS THE WORLD—OUR COUNTRYMEN ARE MANKIND. [SATURDAY, MAY 28, 1831.

fire into which it has fallen;—but urge me not to use moderation in a cause like the present. I am in earnest—I will not equivocate—I will not excuse—I will not retreat a single inch—AND I WILL BE HEARD.

—From William Lloyd Garrison, "To the Public." In The Liberator, *1 January 1831. Reprinted in Wendell Phillips Garrison,* William Lloyd Garrison, 1805–1879: The Story of His Life, Told by His Children. *Vol. 1. New York: The Century Company, 1885.*

THINK ABOUT THIS

How did Garrison use metaphor to persuade his readers?

Angelina Grimké Tells the Truth

Angelina Grimké, the daughter of a slaveholder, was born in Charleston, South Carolina, in 1805. From a young age she witnessed harsh treatment of slaves and grew to hate the

Angelina Grimké (1805–1879) was not only a devoted abolitionist but also an early campaigner for women's equality. She and her sister, Sarah, believed that abolition and women's rights were both part of the greater cause of human rights.

practice of slavery. As young women, she and her sister Sarah moved north and vowed to speak out—in fact, they were among the first female abolitionists. In 1836 Angelina wrote a pamphlet titled *Appeal to the Christian Women of the South,* in which she called on Southern women to join the antislavery movement. Sarah wrote a similar work, addressed to clergy. Officials in South Carolina burned the pamphlets and warned the Grimké sisters that they would be arrested if they attempted to return to Charleston. The Grimkés' activities also drew criticism from men in the North, who believed women shouldn't be involved in politics, or even engage in public speaking. Undaunted, the sisters simply enlarged the scope of their activism to become advocates for women's rights. Following is a portion of Angelina Grimké's *Appeal to the Christian Women of the South.*

IT IS THROUGH THE TONGUE, THE PEN, AND THE PRESS, that truth is principally propagated [spread]. Speak then to your relatives, your friends, your acquaintances on the subject of slavery; be not afraid if you are conscientiously convinced it is *sinful,* to say so openly, but calmly, and to let your sentiments be known. If you are served by the slaves of others, try to ameliorate [ease] their conditions as much as possible; never aggravate their faults, and thus add fuel to the fire of anger already kindled. . . . Discountenance [disapprove of] all cruelty to them, all starvation, all corporal chastisement; these may brutalize and *break* their spirits, but will never bend them to willing, cheerful obedience. If possible, see that they are comfortably and seasonably fed, whether in the house or the field; it is unreasonable and cruel to expect slaves to wait for their breakfast until eleven o'clock, when they rise at five or six. Do all you can, to induce their owners to clothe them well, and then allow them many little indulgences which would contribute to their comfort. Above all, try to persuade your husband, father, brothers, and sons, *that slavery is a crime against God and man,* and that it is a great sin to keep *human beings* in such abject ignorance; to deny them the privilege of learning to read and write. . . .

Some of you *own* slaves yourselves. If you believe slavery is *sinful,* set them at liberty, "undo the heavy burdens and let the oppressed go free." If they wish to remain with you, pay them wages, if not let them leave you. Should they remain teach them, and have them taught the common branches of an English education; they have minds and those minds *ought to be improved.*

—*From Angelina E. Grimké,* Appeal to the Christian Women of the South. *New York: New York Anti-Slavery Society, 1836. Available online at: http://history.furman.edu/~benson/docs/grimke2.htm*

Think about This

1. Do you think many Southern women would have wanted to follow Grimké's advice?
2. Grimké encouraged women to teach slaves to read and write. Why were slaves kept in ignorance?

Frederick Douglass: "This Fourth of July Is Yours, Not Mine"

Writer, abolitionist, and fugitive slave, Frederick Douglass was also a gifted orator who inspired and captivated his audiences. "I shall never forget his speech," recalled William Lloyd Garrison, who heard him at an antislavery convention. "I think I never hated slavery so intensely as at that moment." Born into slavery, Douglass escaped in 1838, when he was about twenty years old. By the 1850s he was traveling around the country to lecture. His firsthand experience with slavery, his impassioned language, and his thunderous voice made him a powerful and effective advocate for emancipation. On July 5, 1852, the Ladies Antislavery Society in Rochester, New York, asked Douglass to give a speech commemorating the signing of the Declaration of Independence. Douglass agreed, but his words would take aim at the values and history that Americans held most sacred. "Fellow-citizens, pardon me, allow me to ask, why am I called upon to speak here to-day?" Douglass said to those gathered to hear him. "This Fourth of July is yours, not mine. You may rejoice, I must mourn." Following is a passage from this famous speech.

Frederick Douglass (*seated, left, at the table*) at an outdoor antislavery meeting around 1845. Douglass was a moving and persuasive writer and speaker, who did much to further the cause of abolition.

WHAT, TO THE AMERICAN SLAVE, IS YOUR 4TH OF JULY? I answer: a day that reveals to him, more than all other days in the year, the gross injustice and cruelty to which he is the constant victim. To him, your celebration is a sham; your boasted liberty, an unholy license; your national greatness, swelling vanity; your sounds of rejoicing are empty and heartless; your denunciations of tyrants, brass fronted impudence; your shouts of liberty and equality, hollow mockery; your prayers and hymns, your sermons and thanksgivings, with all your religious parade, and solemnity, are, to him, mere bombast, fraud, deception, impiety, and hypocrisy—a thin veil to cover up crimes which would disgrace a nation of savages.

"The existence of slavery in this country brands your republicanism as a sham, your humanity as a base pretence, and your Christianity as a lie."

There is not a nation on the earth guilty of practices, more shocking and bloody, than are the people of these United States, at this very hour.

. . . The existence of slavery in this country brands your republicanism as a sham, your humanity as a base pretence, and your Christianity as a lie. It destroys your moral power abroad; it corrupts your politicians at home. It saps the foundation of religion; it makes your name a hissing, and a by word to a mocking earth. It is the antagonistic force in your government, the only thing that seriously disturbs and endangers your Union.

—From Frederick Douglass, "What to the Slave Is the Fourth of July?"
In The Oxford Frederick Douglass Reader. *Edited by William L. Andrews.*
New York: Oxford University Press, 1997.

Think about This

How did Douglass' use of the pronoun *your* help to make his point about African Americans having no part in the American dream?

John Brown's Insurrection

A white abolitionist named John Brown planned a raid on the armory in Harper's Ferry, Virginia. He hoped that his actions would encourage slaves to join in the rebellion and that he would soon have an army of sufficient force, as well as weapons from the armory, to fight for their emancipation. On October 16, 1859, Brown put his plan into action. He and twenty-one men successfully seized the armory and took sixty people hostage. But no slaves came to support

Frank Leslie's Illustrated Newspaper, an important primary source for nineteenth-century American history, published this engraving of John Brown's raid on Harper's Ferry three weeks after it occurred.

him. The local militia and then the marines ultimately put an end to the insurrection, leaving ten of Brown's men dead, including two of his sons. John Brown, along with six others, was captured. Five managed to escape. The captives were quickly tried for treason, insurrection, and murder (although Brown claimed he had not murdered anyone). They were found guilty and sentenced to death.

At first people were shocked by John Brown's violent action, but soon many Northerners began to speak of him as a hero, especially after learning about his address to the court. The insurrection, though not successful in the way Brown had hoped, is believed to have hastened the march toward civil war—and ultimately emancipation. Following is a portion of Brown's speech to the court.

HAD I INTERFERED IN THE MANNER WHICH I ADMIT, and which I admit has been fairly proved (for I admire the truthfulness and candor of the greater portion of the witnesses who have testified in this case),—had I so interfered in behalf of the rich, the powerful, the intelligent, the so-called great, or in behalf of any of their friends—either father, mother, sister, wife, or children, or any of that class—and suffered and sacrificed what I have in this interference, it would have been all right; and every man in this court would have deemed it an act worthy of reward rather than punishment.

The court acknowledges, as I suppose, the validity of the law of God. I see a book kissed here which I suppose to be the Bible. . . . That teaches me that all things whatsoever I would that men should do to me, I should do even so to them. It teaches me further to "remember them that are in bonds, as bound with them." I endeavored to act up to that instruction. . . . I believe that to have interfered as I have done—as I have always freely admitted I have

John Brown Going to His Hanging, painted in 1942 by African-American artist Horace Pippin

done—in behalf of His despised poor, was not wrong, but right. Now if it is deemed necessary that I should forfeit my life for the furtherance of the ends of justice, and mingle my blood further with the blood of my children and with the blood of millions in this slave country whose rights are disregarded by wicked, cruel, and unjust enactments.—I submit; so let it be done!

—From "Address of John Brown to the Virginia Court at Charles Town, Virginia" on November 2, 1859. Available online at: http://www.pbs.org/wgbh/aia/part4/4h2943t.html

Think about This

1. What did Brown say would have been worthy of reward rather than punishment?
2. Brown referred to the Bible as justification for his actions. What biblical concept was he referring to?

After the Emancipation Proclamation went into effect in 1863, many slaves fled their plantations and took refuge behind the Union army's lines.

Chapter 7

Free at Last: Emancipation

DURING THE 1850s the interests of North and South would collide more violently than ever. Several events hastened the arrival of what seemed inevitable—a civil war. In early 1854 Senator Stephen A. Douglas of Illinois introduced the Kansas-Nebraska bill to the Senate. After much debate, first in the Senate and then in the House, the bill was passed. The new law allowed these two territories—and any that came after—to enter the Union with or without slavery, as decided by the vote of the people who lived there. Douglas's main intent was to appease slave states, and at first Americans North and South believed the law would help to lessen tensions. After all, it seemed democratic: the people would decide the issue for themselves. The Kansas-Nebraska Act did not ease hostility, however; it only ignited new animosity.

Nebraska was too far north to attract many slaveholders, but Kansas became a battleground between pro- and antislavery forces. Groups on both sides began to rally supporters to settle in the territory, hoping to tilt the population's balance, and ultimately the territorial elections, in their favor. Violence soon erupted. Proslavery factions destroyed the free-soil town of Lawrence; in retaliation, abolitionist John Brown, five years before leading his own insurrection, killed five proslavery settlers in the region, opening up a period of violent clashes that left two hundred people dead.

In March 1855 elections to the territory's legislature were held. Mobs of slaveholders from neighboring Missouri and Arkansas entered Kansas, took over the polling places, drove the real settlers away from the polls, and cast their votes in favor of proslavery candidates. Although only some 2,900 settlers were eligible to vote, at election's end, more than 6,300 ballots had been counted.

At about the same time, a slave's lawsuit was to be heard by the Supreme Court. In the 1830s a Missouri slave named Dred Scott had been taken by his master, an officer with the U.S. Army, to live in the free states of Illinois and Wisconsin. The army ordered Scott's owner back to Missouri, and he and Scott returned to the slave state, where his master later died. Scott learned that his extended stay in the free states meant that he could claim his freedom. In 1846, with the help of abolitionists, he sued for his freedom in court, claiming he should be free because he had lived on free soil for a long time. After more than ten years of appeals, the case went all the way to the U.S. Supreme Court. In March 1857 Scott lost the decision when the Court declared that no slave or descendant of a slave had ever been a U.S. citizen. As a noncitizen, Scott had no rights and could not sue in federal court. He therefore was not entitled to his freedom. The Court's ruling had an impact on the lives of every African American in the United

States, both enslaved and free. It also took the nation one step closer to civil war.

In 1858 a politician from Illinois, Abraham Lincoln, was beginning to make a name for himself at the national level. As the Republican candidate for the U.S. Senate, Lincoln challenged the incumbent, Stephen Douglas, to a series of debates. Topics would include the status of Kansas, the future of slavery, and, perhaps, the future of the Union itself. With Lincoln a critic of slavery's spread to new parts of the nation and Douglas the author of the Kansas-Nebraska Act, the debates promised to be tense and dramatic. Journalists from all over the country came to observe and report. Although Lincoln lost the election, the debates made him famous—so famous that the Republican Party selected him as its presidential candidate for the election of 1860. He won, with votes cast in his favor almost exclusively by Northerners. Less than two months later, South Carolina seceded from the Union.

Dred Scott was sold shortly after the Supreme Court decision on his case, but his new owner gave him his freedom. Scott did not live to see the rest of the slaves freed, however; he died in 1858.

Ten more Southern states quickly followed South Carolina's

example. Together these eleven states comprised what they hoped would be a new nation, the Confederate States of America. The decades-old threat of a nation divided had finally come to pass, and by April 1861, the Civil War (1861–1865) had begun. Four years of brutal conflict eventually led to a Northern victory, preserving the Union intact. The North's triumph had many repercussions, but perhaps none was more critical than emancipation—an outcome of the war that would grant freedom to four million African Americans.

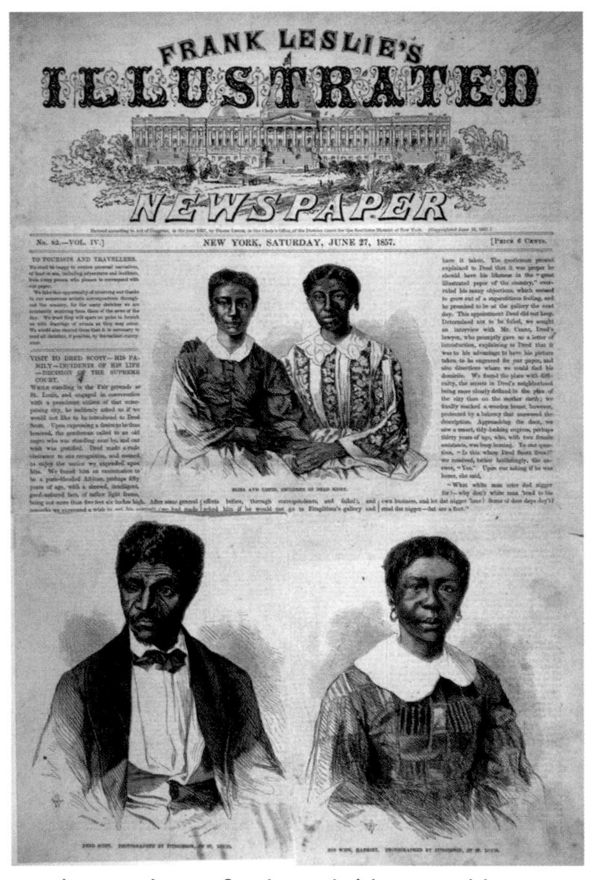
FRANK LESLIE'S
ILLUSTRATED
NEWSPAPER

NEW YORK, SATURDAY, JUNE 27, 1857.

Dred Scott, his wife, their children, and his story were featured on the front page of *Frank Leslie's Illustrated Newspaper* on June 27, 1857.

The Dred Scott Case

The Dred Scott case was heard by the Supreme Court in 1857, but to many it was clear that Scott had lost the case before the Court ever considered it. Seven of the justices had been appointed by proslavery presidents, and five of these came from slaveholding families; their opinion was bound to be biased. Following is the Court's decision, written by Chief Justice Roger B. Taney, a staunch supporter of slavery.

THE QUESTION IS SIMPLY THIS: Can a negro, whose ancestors were imported into this country, and sold as slaves, become a member of the political community formed and brought into existence by the Constitution of the United States, and as such become entitled to all the rights, and privileges, and immunities, guaranteed by that instrument to the citizen? One of which rights is the privilege of suing in a court of the United States in the cases specified in the Constitution. . . .

. . . We think they are not, and that [people of African origin] are not included, and were not intended to be included, under the word "citizens" in the Constitution, and can therefore claim none of the rights and privileges which that instrument provides for and secures to citizens of the United States. On the contrary, they were at that time considered as a subordinate and inferior class of beings. . . .

"We think . . . that [people of African origin] . . . were not intended to be included under the word 'citizens' in the Constitution."

They had for more than a century before [the Constitution was written] been regarded as . . . altogether unfit to associate with the white race, either in social or political relations; and so far inferior, that they had no rights which the white man was bound to respect; and that the negro might justly and lawfully be reduced to slavery. . . .

And upon a full and careful consideration of the subject, the court is of opinion, that . . . Dred Scott was not a citizen of Missouri within the meaning of the Constitution of the United States, and not entitled as such to sue in its courts. . . .

. . . [Furthermore,] as Scott was a slave when taken into the State of Illinois by his owner, and was there held as such, and brought back in that character, his status, as free or slave, depended on the laws of Missouri [a slave state], and not of Illinois. . . .

—*From* Dred Scott v. Sanford. *Text available online at http://www.pbs.org/wgbh/aia/part4/4h2933t.html*

Think about This

1. Did the Court believe that Scott was entitled to bring a case to trial?
2. Why does the chief justice discuss how people of African origin were viewed at the time the Constitution was written?
3. According to the Court, why wasn't Scott free?

A House Divided

Although Lincoln believed slavery was wrong, for most of his career he did not believe it should be abolished completely. He knew that any attempt to end slavery would seriously threaten the Union, so his goal was to keep the practice from spreading to new areas. But Lincoln also began to fear that slavery might one day exist in every state. In June 1858, accepting the nomination as the Republican candidate for the U.S. Senate, he gave a famous speech, an excerpt of which follows.

WE ARE NOW FAR INTO THE FIFTH YEAR since a policy [the Kansas-Nebraska Act] was initiated with the avowed object, and confident promise, of putting an end to slavery agitation. Under the operation of that policy, that agitation has not only not ceased, but has constantly augmented. In my opinion, it will not cease, until a crisis shall have been reached and passed. "A house divided against itself cannot stand." I believe this government cannot endure permanently half slave and half free. I do not expect the Union to be dissolved—I do not expect the house to fall—but I do expect it will cease to be divided. It will become all one thing, or all the other. Either the opponents of slavery will arrest the further spread of it, and place it where the public mind shall rest in the belief that it is in the course of ultimate extinction; or its advocates will push it forward, till it shall become alike lawful in all the States, old as well as new—North as well as South.

"I do not expect the house to fall."

Although Lincoln lost his bid for the U.S. Senate in 1858, he went on, two years later, to battle for the presidency. This political cartoon from 1860 depicts Lincoln and Douglas as a pair of prize fighters—the prize being the White House.

Have we no tendency to the latter condition?

Let any one who doubts carefully contemplate [the] legal combination . . . of the Nebraska doctrine and the Dred Scott decision. . .

The new year of 1854 found slavery excluded from more than half the States by State constitutions, and from most of the national territory by congressional prohibition. Four days later commenced the struggle which ended in repealing that congressional prohibition. This opened all the national territory to slavery. . . .

The several points of the Dred Scott decision, in connection with Senator Douglas's . . . policy, constitute the piece of machinery, in its present state of advancement. . . . The working points of that machinery are:

Firstly, That no negro slave imported as such from Africa, and descendant of such slave, can ever be a citizen of any State, in the sense of that term as used in the Constitution of the United States. . . .

Secondly, That, "subject to the Constitution of the United States," neither Congress nor a Territorial Legislature can exclude slavery from any United States Territory. This point is made in order that individual men fill up the Territories with slaves, without danger of losing them as property, and thus to enhance the chances of permanency to the institution through all the future.

Thirdly, That whether the holding a negro in actual slavery in a free State makes him free, as against the holder, the United States courts will not decide, but will leave to be decided by the courts of any slave state the negro may be forced into by the master. . . . what Dred Scott's master might lawfully do with Dred Scott, in the free State of Illinois, every other master may lawfully do with any other one, or one thousand slaves, in Illinois, or in any other free State.

—From Abraham Lincoln, "House Divided" Speech at Springfield, Illinois, June 16, 1858. In Abraham Lincoln: Speeches and Writings 1832–1858. *Edited by Don E. Fehrenbacher. New York: Library of America, 1989.*

Think about This

1. What did Lincoln believe was the result of the Kansas-Nebraska Act?
2. What did he predict might happen in the future?
3. What was the purpose of the "machinery" that Lincoln referred to?

A More Perfect Union: South Carolina Is the First to Secede

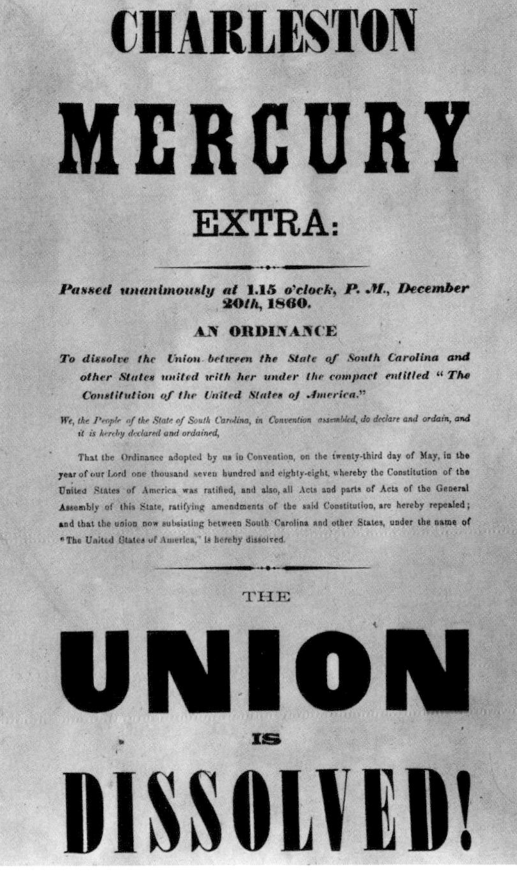

CHARLESTON

MERCURY

EXTRA:

Passed unanimously at 1.15 o'clock, P. M., December 20th, 1860.

AN ORDINANCE

To dissolve the Union between the State of South Carolina and other States united with her under the compact entitled "The Constitution of the United States of America."

We, the People of the State of South Carolina, in Convention assembled, do declare and ordain, and it is hereby declared and ordained,

That the Ordinance adopted by us in Convention, on the twenty-third day of May, in the year of our Lord one thousand seven hundred and eighty-eight, whereby the Constitution of the United States of America was ratified, and also, all Acts and parts of Acts of the General Assembly of this State, ratifying amendments of the said Constitution, are hereby repealed; and that the union now subsisting between South Carolina and other States, under the name of "The United States of America," is hereby dissolved.

THE

UNION

IS

DISSOLVED!

A broadside from Charleston, South Carolina, announces the state's secession from the Union, December 20, 1860.

Lincoln was elected president on November 6, 1860, and by the end of the following month, South Carolina had seceded from the Union. The following year most of the slave states would follow suit; only Delaware, Kentucky, Maryland, and Missouri would remain in the Union. The seceding states formed the Confederate States of America. At his inauguration in March of 1861, Lincoln urged the Confederates not to start a civil war, saying they had no right "to destroy the government, while I shall have the most solemn one to preserve, protect, and defend it." But when, in April, Confederates attacked Fort Sumter, a Union garrison off the coast of South Carolina, the war began. It would be the bloodiest in the nation's history, ultimately taking the lives of more than 600,000 Americans—some fighting for constitutional principles, others for moral ideals, some to preserve states' rights, others to preserve the Union. Following is a selection from the South Carolina declaration of secession.

THE ENDS FOR WHICH THE CONSTITUTION WAS FRAMED are declared by itself to be "to form a more perfect union, establish justice, insure domestic tranquility, provide for the common defence, promote the general welfare, and secure the blessings of liberty to ourselves and our posterity."

These ends it endeavored to accomplish by a Federal Government, in which each State was recognized as an equal, and had separate control over its own institutions. The right of property in slaves was recognized by giving to free persons distinct political rights, by giving them the right to represent [representation], and burthening [burdening] them with direct taxes for three-fifths of their slaves; by authorizing the importation of slaves for twenty years; and by stipulating for the rendition of fugitives from labor.

rendition
surrender

We affirm that these ends for which this Government was instituted have been defeated, and the Government itself has been made destructive of them by the action of the non-slaveholding States. Those States have assumed the right of deciding upon the propriety of our domestic institutions; and have denied the rights of property established in fifteen of the States and recognized by the Constitution; they have denounced as sinful the institution of slavery; they have permitted open establishment among them of societies, whose avowed object is to disturb the peace and to [take] the property of the citizens of other States. They have encouraged and assisted thousands of our slaves to leave their homes; and those who remain,

propriety
properness

have been incited by emissaries, books and pictures to servile insurrection.

. . . A geographical line has been drawn across the Union, and all the States north of that line have united in the election of a man to the high office of President of the United States, whose opinions and purposes are hostile to slavery. He is to be entrusted with the administration of the common Government, because he has declared that that "Government cannot endure permanently half slave, half free," and that the public mind must rest in the belief that slavery is in the course of ultimate extinction. . . .

"A geographical line has been drawn across the Union."

We, therefore, the People of South Carolina . . . have solemnly declared that the Union heretofore existing between this State and the other States of North America, is dissolved, and that the State of South Carolina has resumed her position among the nations of the world, as a separate and independent State; with full power to levy war, conclude peace, contract alliances, establish commerce, and to do all other acts and things which independent States may of right do.

—From the South Carolina Declaration of Secession, December 1860. Available online at: http://www.yale.edu/lawweb/avalon/csa/scarsec.htm

Think about This

1. Which parts of the Constitution does the declaration use to justify the decision to leave the Union? Is the argument it puts forth a logical one?
2. The declaration quotes Lincoln's "House Divided" speech. How do you think Southerners interpreted the quotation in light of Lincoln's election to the presidency?

Forever Free: A Proclamation Changes the Course of War

In the early years of the war, the Confederacy appeared to be en route to victory. With exceptional military leadership, it won most of the battles. Lincoln had never claimed that the war was being fought to free the slaves, but to preserve the Union. As the war progressed, however, growing deadlier each month, he saw reason to change the character of the war—to state directly that it was intended to bring about emancipation. For one thing, more Northerners were turning against slavery, and he no longer risked losing significant support for the war. In addition, he believed European nations, many of which disapproved of slavery, might be more willing to help the Union if he admitted that the slaves' freedom was at stake. Finally, many slaves were running away from their masters. As freedmen, they could enlist in the Union army—something they might be more willing to do knowing that a Union victory would mean an end to slavery. With these factors in mind, Lincoln

One of the approximately 180,000 African-American men who served in the Union army. Two-thirds of these soldiers were ex-slaves.

decided to issue the Emancipation Proclamation. As you read the excerpt here, keep in mind that four slaveholding states remained in the Union.

BY THE PRESIDENT OF THE UNITED STATES OF AMERICA:
A PROCLAMATION.

Whereas, on the twenty-second day of September, in the year of our Lord one thousand eight hundred and sixty-two, a proclamation was issued by the President of the United States, containing, among other things, the following, to wit:

That on the first day of January, in the year of our Lord one thousand eight hundred and sixty-three, all persons held as slaves within any State or designated part of a State, the people whereof shall then be in rebellion against the United States, shall be then, thenceforward, and forever free; and the Executive Government of the United States, including the military and naval authority thereof, will recognize and maintain the freedom of such persons, and will do no act or acts to repress such persons, or any of them, in any efforts they may make for their actual freedom.

From the Emancipation Proclamation, January 1, 1863. Text available online at http://www.nps.gov/ncro/anti/emancipation.html

Think about This

1. The Emancipation Proclamation frees only slaves in states where the people are "in rebellion against the United States." What does this mean?
2. Why didn't Lincoln free all the slaves?
3. Do you think the Emancipation Proclamation actually did free any slaves?

Freedom! The Thirteenth Amendment Ends Slavery

The year 1863 brought the Union army more victories, and by the time Lincoln began his second term as president in 1865, the end of the war was in sight. Lincoln now turned his thoughts to putting an end to slavery in America forever. He took an active role in getting the Thirteenth Amendment, the text of which appears below, passed. He also supported congressmen who insisted that at war's end, no Southern state could return to the Union without adopting the amendment. Although Lincoln looked forward to rebuilding the nation after the long, painful years of war, it was not to be. Five days after Confederate general Robert E. Lee surrendered to Union general Ulysses S. Grant, Lincoln was assassinated.

AMENDMENT XIII

SECTION 1.
Neither slavery nor involuntary servitude, except as a punishment for crime whereof the party shall have been duly convicted, shall exist within the United States, or any place subject to their jurisdiction.

SECTION 2.
Congress shall have power to enforce this article by appropriate legislation.

—The Thirteenth Amendment to the Constitution, passed by Congress January 31, 1865; ratified December 6, 1865. Available online at: http://memory.loc.gov/const/const.html

Think about This

Why do you think the second section of the amendment was necessary? To what type of legislation might this refer?

"The Niggers Will Catch Hell": A Northern Official Describes Life after the War

What was life like for African Americans following the war? Had freedom greatly improved their lives? Certainly freedom was better than bondage. Following the Thirteenth Amendment, two more amendments were passed that also held the promise of great change. The Fourteenth Amendment gave the rights of citizenship to all people born (or naturalized) in the United States, effectively overturning the effects of the Dred Scott decision. It also prohibited individual states from taking away these rights. The Fifteenth Amendment granted suffrage—the right to vote—to black men. (Women of all races would not be permitted to vote until 1920.) But opinion among the majority of the people of the South was not transformed by the events of the war, the Emancipation Proclamation, or the Civil War amendments to the Constitution. The South lay in ruins, and the prejudice and ill will that had existed prior to the conflict were only intensified by the devastation it had caused. In the years following the war, Northerners ran the governments of the South and worked to ensure the safety of the former slaves, but over time the state governments would return to the hands of white Southerners. It was unlikely that blacks would be treated as equals in a land where they were once

After the Civil War, most African Americans who stayed in the South continued the plantation work they had done as slaves. As tenant farmers, sharecroppers, or laborers, they often lived in poverty, with little opportunity to enjoy their new-won freedom. It would be another century before African Americans began to achieve full equality and civil rights.

considered property. In the following passage, a Northern official working at the Freedmen's Bureau describes African-American lives in the post–Civil War South.

WHEREVER I GO—the street, the shop, the house, or the steamboat—I hear the people talk in such a way as to indicate that they are yet unable to conceive of the Negro as possessing any rights at all. Men who are honorable in their dealings with their white neighbors will cheat a Negro without feeling a single twinge of their honor. To kill a Negro they do not deem murder; to debauch a Negro woman they do not think fornication; to take the property away from a Negro they do not consider robbery. The people boast that when they get freedmen affairs in their own hands, to use their own classic expression, "the niggers will catch hell."

"To kill a Negro they do not deem murder."

The reason of all this is simple and manifest. The whites esteem the blacks their property by natural right, and however much they may admit that the individual relations of masters and slaves have been destroyed by the war and the President's emancipation proclamation, they still have an ingrained feeling that the blacks at large belong to the whites at large, and whenever opportunity serves they treat the colored people just as their profit, caprice or passion may dictate.

—From Colonel Samuel Thomas, Assistant Commissioner, Bureau of Refugees, Freedmen and Abandoned Lands, in 39 Cong., 1 Sess., Senate Exec. Doc. 2 (1865). Available online at: http://www.digitalhistory.uh.edu/black_voices/voices_display.cfm?id=82

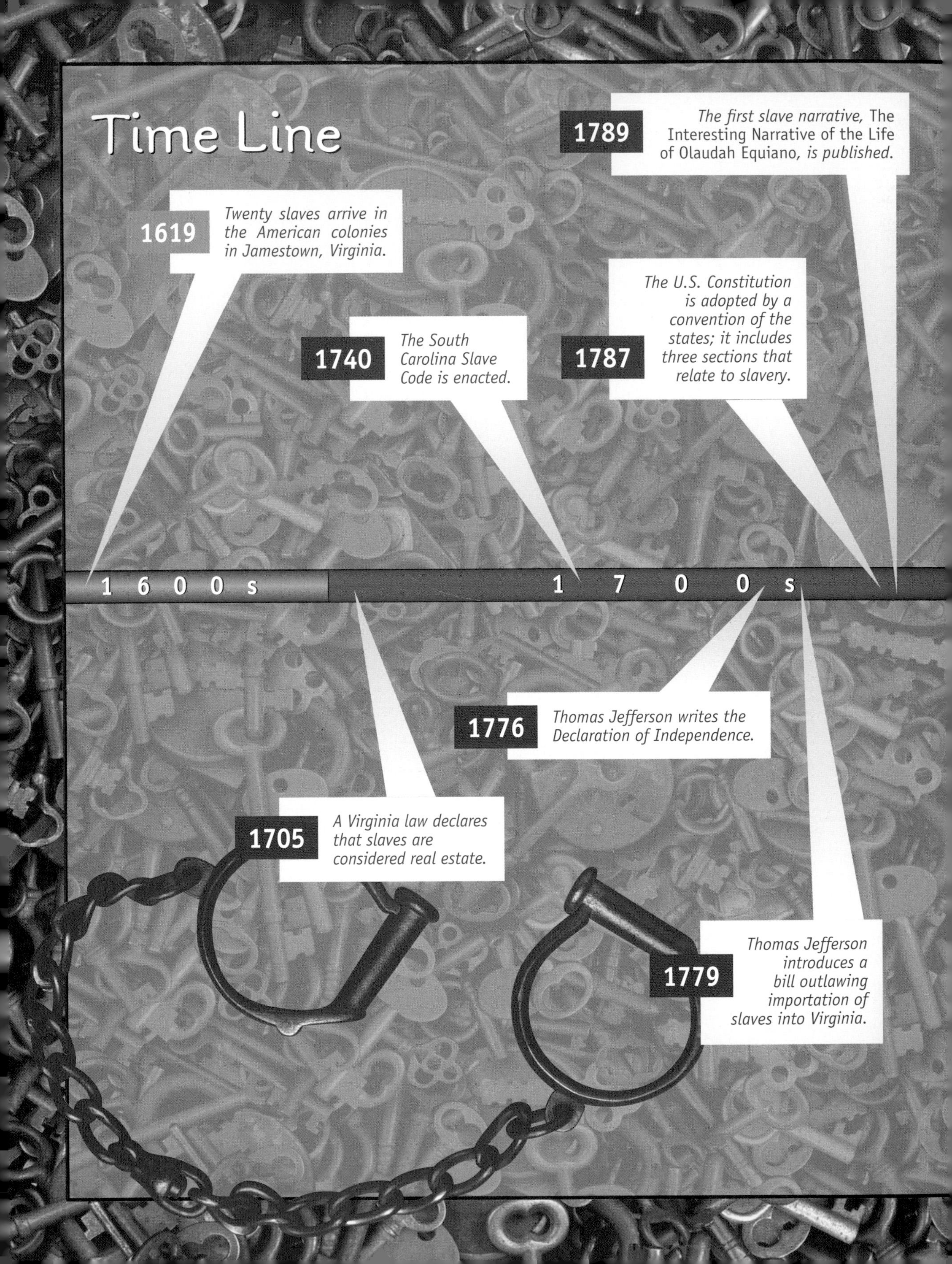

Time Line
1619 Twenty slaves arrive in the American colonies in Jamestown, Virginia.
1705 A Virginia law declares that slaves are considered real estate.
1740 The South Carolina Slave Code is enacted.
1776 Thomas Jefferson writes the Declaration of Independence.
1779 Thomas Jefferson introduces a bill outlawing importation of slaves into Virginia.
1787 The U.S. Constitution is adopted by a convention of the states; it includes three sections that relate to slavery.
1789 The first slave narrative, The Interesting Narrative of the Life of Olaudah Equiano, is published.
1600s
1700s

Any holder but A Slaveholder

Any holder but A Slave Holder

1831

JANUARY 1
William Lloyd Garrison publishes the first issue of The Liberator*.*

AUGUST
Nat Turner leads a slave revolt in Southampton County, Virginia.

1 8 0 0 s →

1808

An act of Congress abolishes the slave trade.

1836

Abolitionist Angelina Grimké publishes Appeal to the Christian Women of the South.

1845

Narrative of the Life of Frederick Douglass *is published.*

1848

Ellen and William Craft escape to the North using public transportation.

1849

Henry Brown escapes by shipping himself to Philadelphia.

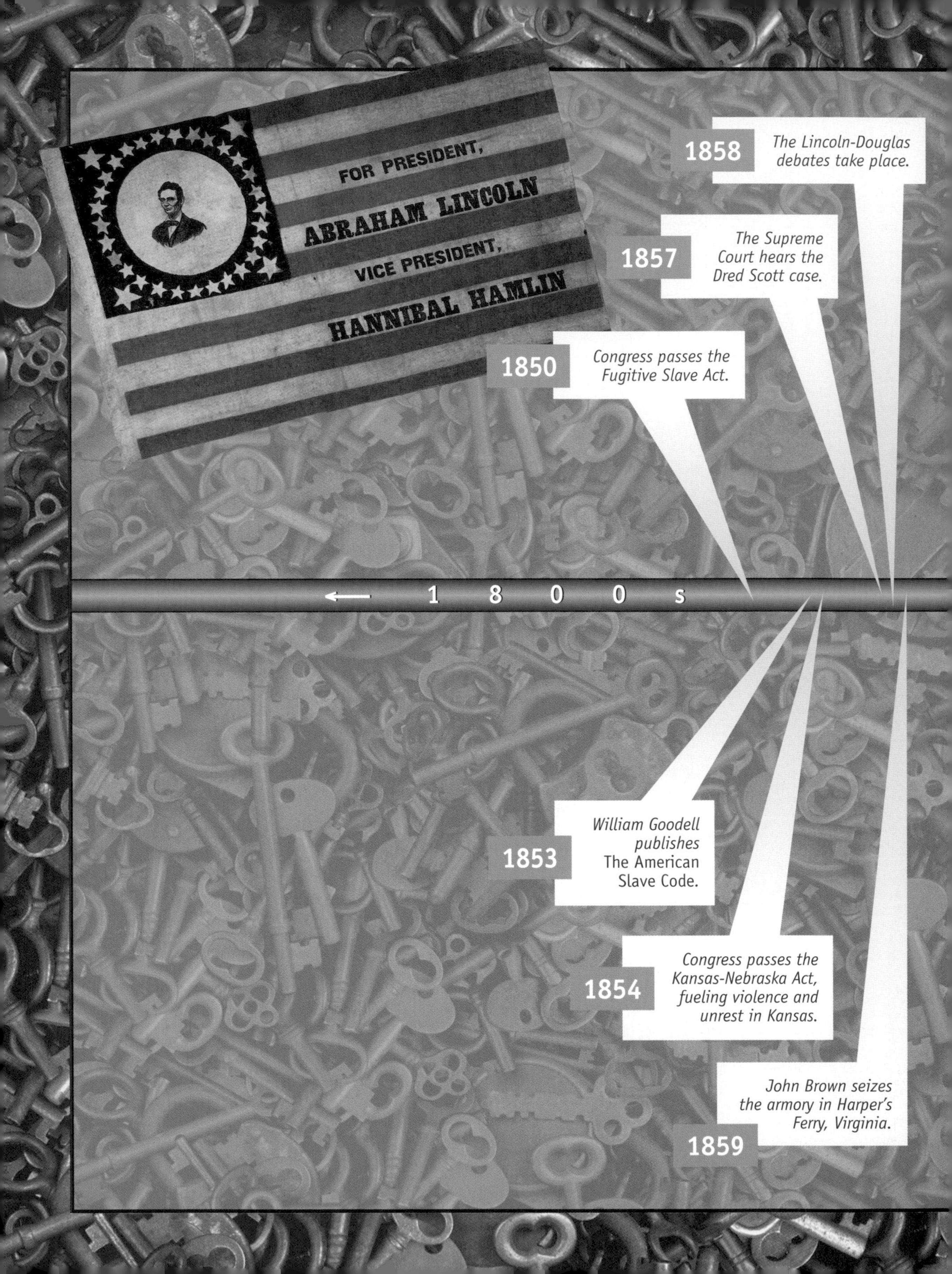
FOR PRESIDENT,
ABRAHAM LINCOLN
VICE PRESIDENT,
HANNIBAL HAMLIN
1858 The Lincoln-Douglas debates take place.
1857 The Supreme Court hears the Dred Scott case.
1850 Congress passes the Fugitive Slave Act.
1800s
1853 William Goodell publishes The American Slave Code.
1854 Congress passes the Kansas-Nebraska Act, fueling violence and unrest in Kansas.
1859 John Brown seizes the armory in Harper's Ferry, Virginia.

1860

NOVEMBER 6
Abraham Lincoln is elected president.

DECEMBER 20
South Carolina is the first state to secede from the Union.

1861

The Civil War begins when the Confederates attack Fort Sumter.

1863

The Emancipation Proclamation becomes law on January 1.

1864

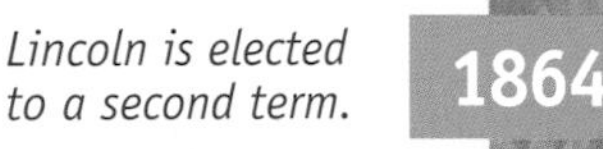

Lincoln is elected to a second term.

1865

JANUARY 31
Congress passes the Thirteenth Amendment.

APRIL 9
Confederate general Robert E. Lee surrenders at Appomattox Courthouse, Virginia.

APRIL 14
Lincoln is assassinated.

DECEMBER 6
The Thirteenth Amendment is ratified.

1900s

1936–1940

The Federal Writers' Project conducts more than 2,300 interviews with former slaves.

Glossary

abolitionist a person who sought to end the practice of slavery in the United States

chattel an article of movable personal property

civil rights a citizen's rights of personal liberty, guaranteed in the United States by the Constitution

contradiction a situation in which factors or actions are inconsistent with or contrary to one another

cotton gin a machine that separates the seeds, hulls, and other material from cotton

emancipate to free

incumbent the current holder of an office

insurrection a rebellion or revolt

quarantine to isolate a person or thing in an attempt to avoid spreading a contagious disease

radical having to do with an extreme viewpoint; a person who seeks to make extreme changes to conditions or institutions

secede to withdraw

To Find Out More

BOOKS

Beller, Susan Provost. *American Voices from the Civil War.* New York: Benchmark Books, 2003.

Equiano, Olaudah. *The Interesting Narrative and Other Writings.* Edited by Vincent Caretta. New York: Penguin, 2003.

Feelings, Tom. *The Middle Passage: White Ships, Black Cargo.* New York: Dial Books for Young Readers, 1995.

Gates, Henry Louis, Jr. *The Classic Slave Narratives.* New York: Signet Classic, 2002. (Includes *The Life of Olaudah Equiano; The History of Mary Prince; Narrative of the Life of Frederick Douglass;* and *Incidents in the Life of a Slave Girl* [Harriet Jacobs].)

January, Brendan. *The Dred Scott Decision.* Chicago: Children's Press, 1998.

Lester, Julius. *To Be a Slave.* New York: Dial Books for Young Readers, 1998.

Lyons, Mary E. *Letters from a Slave Girl: The Story of Harriet Jacobs.* New York: Simon Pulse, 1996.

McKissack, Patricia. *A Picture of Freedom: The Diary of Clotee, a Slave Girl, Belmont Plantation, 1859.* Dear America series. New York: Scholastic, 1997. (Fiction.)

McKissack, Patricia. *The Rebels against Slavery: Story of American Slave Revolts.* New York: Scholastic, 1996.

Paulsen, Gary. *Nightjohn.* New York: Delacorte, 1993. (Fiction.)

Roberts, Russell. *Lincoln and the Abolition of Slavery.* San Diego: Lucent Books, 2000.

Ruggiero, Adriane. *American Voices from Reconstruction.* New York: Benchmark Books, 2007.

Thomas, Velma Maia. *Lest We Forget: The Passage from Africa to Slavery and Emancipation.* New York: Crown, 1997. (A three-dimensional interactive book with photographs and documents from the Black Holocaust Exhibit.)

Waldstreicher, David. *The Struggle against Slavery: A History in Documents.* New York: Oxford University Press, 2002.

Yetman, Norman R., editor. *Voices from Slavery: 100 Authentic Narratives.* Enlarged edition. Minneola, NY: Dover, 2000.

WEB SITES

The Web sites listed here were in existence in 2005–2006 when this book was being written. Their names or locations may have changed since then.

In general, when using the Internet to do research on a history topic, you should use caution. You will find numerous Web sites that are very attractive to look at and appear to be professional in format. Proceed with caution, however. Many, even the best ones, contain errors. Some Web sites even insert disclaimers or warnings about mistakes that may have made their way into the site. In the case of primary sources, the builders of the Web site often transcribe previously published material, good or bad, accurate or inaccurate. Therefore, you have to judge the content of all Web sites. This requires a critical eye.

A good rule for using the Internet as a resource is always to compare what you find in Web sites to several other sources, such as librarian- or teacher-recommended reference works and major works of scholarship. By doing this, you will discover the myriad versions of history that exist.

Visit the National Archives' page dedicated to the Emancipation Proclamation:

http://www.archives.gov/exhibit_hall/featured_documents/emancipation_proclamation/

To read more of the Federal Writer's Project slave narratives, visit the Library of Congress site devoted to them:

http://memory.loc.gov/ammem/snhtml/snhome.html

View other exhibits at the Library of Congress related to slavery and African Americans:

http://memory.loc.gov.ammem.aaohtml.aohome.html

For more slave narratives and primary sources on slavery, visit the following sites:

http://www.digitalhistory.uh.edu/black_voices/black_voices.cfm

http://docsouth.unc.edu/neh/index.html

http://www.spartacus.schoolnet.co.uk/USAslavery.htm

http://xroads.virginia.edu/~HYPER/wpa/wpahome.html

To learn more about abolitionism in America, visit

http://rmc.library.cornell.edu/abolitionism/index.htm

Visit the excellent PBS Web site *Africans in America* at

http://www.pbs.org/wgbh/aia/home.html

Index

Page numbers for illustrations are in boldface

ABOUT THE AUTHOR

Elizabeth Sirimarco published her first book in 1990. Since that time, she has written books for young people on subjects ranging from tennis to Thomas Jefferson, the Yanomami to the Cold War. "The best thing about writing," she says, "is that I still have the chance to learn new things—it's like being in school again. Kids probably wouldn't understand (I wouldn't have believed it at their age), but I really miss school!" A graduate of the University of Colorado at Boulder, she also earned a degree in Italian from the Università per Stranieri in Siena, Italy. In addition to writing, Elizabeth works as an editor and occasionally enjoys the opportunity to work as an Italian translator. She and her husband David, a photographer, live with a very large dog and a very small cat in Denver, Colorado.